A FOREST OF GIANT OAKS
VOLUME I

INDEPENDENCE

J.M. RASINSKE

H-VEGAS
—PUBLISHING—

WWW.JMRASINSKE.COM

Cover design: Joe Montgomery

Author photo: Jared Lazarus

H-Vegas Publishing logo design: Valentina Álvarez & Catalina Beltrán

ISBN (paperback): 979-8-9874045-1-5

ISBN (ebook): 979-8-9874045-0-8

H-Vegas Publishing

www.jmrasinske.com

First Edition: December 2022

CONTENTS

REVIEW QUOTES

PRAISE FOR A FOREST OF GIANT OAKS VOLUME 1 – INDEPENDENCE

"J.M. Rasinske comes out of the gates at light speed with his debut novel, A Forest of Giant Oaks: Independence. With a page-turning plot intricately woven through multiple timelines, this novel meshes time travel and historical fiction in the best ways possible. Rasinske masterfully brings the Founding Fathers, headlined by the ardent, witty Benjamin Franklin, into the twenty-first century in such an engaging way, while maintaining the historical accuracy of these complex characters. As I finished the last page, I was left with one thought: I'm ready for Volume Two."

- SCOTT BLACKBURN, author of *It Dies With You*

"What if time travel was invented not in the future, but more than two hundred and fifty years in the past? And what if America's founding fathers sent a distress call to our present, seeking help to win the Revolutionary War? The answers to these questions (and more!) explode across the pages of J.M. Rasinkse's Independence, the first volume of his A Forest of Giant Oaks series. With the mind-bending premise of a Blake Crouch thriller combined with the sweeping scope of a Ken Follett historical epic, readers young and old will be riveted as past and present collide. If you like a ripping good yarn, this is the book for you."

   - J.G. HETHERTON, author of *Last Girl Gone* and *What Lies Beneath*

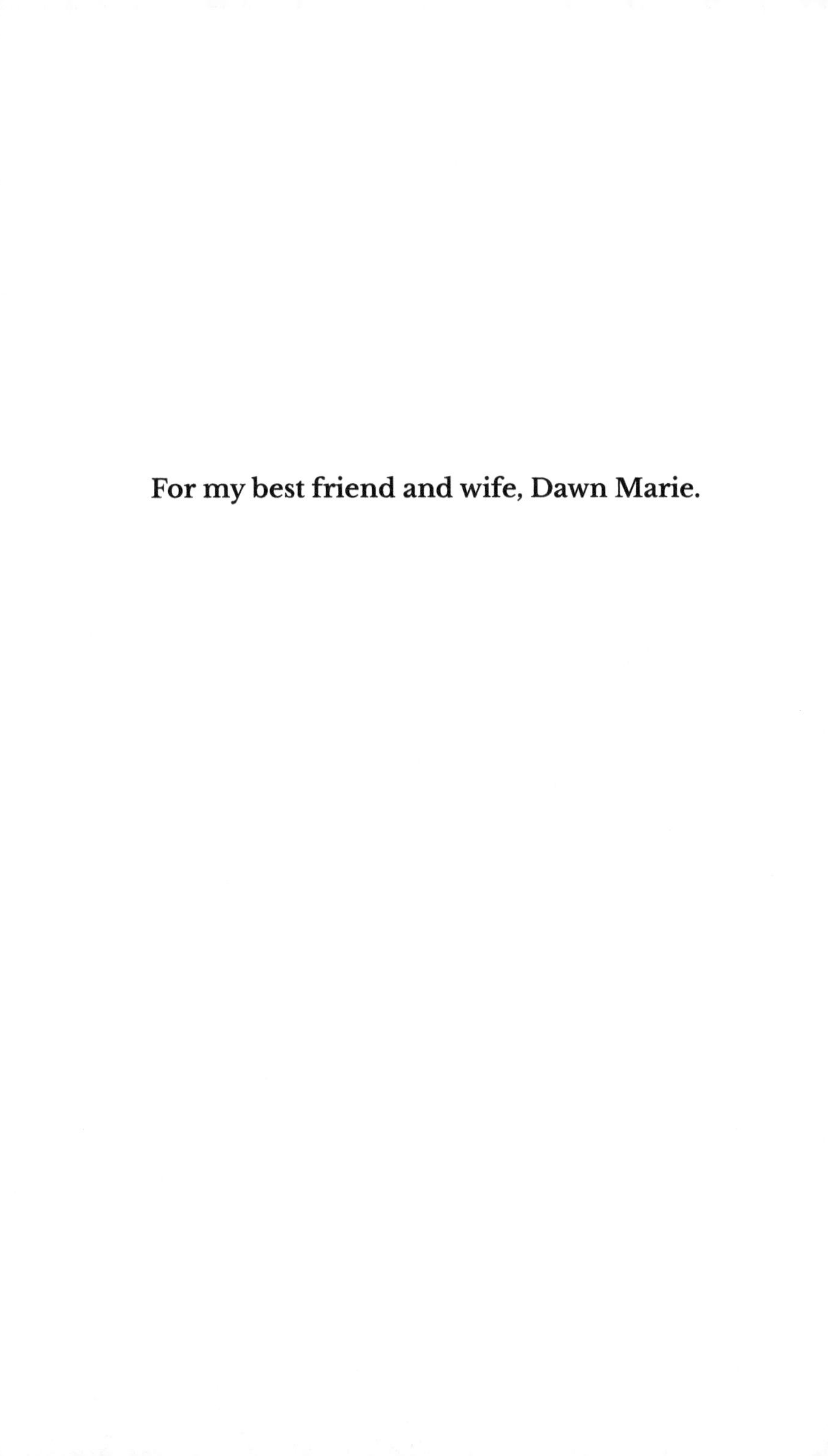

For my best friend and wife, Dawn Marie.

CHAPTER ONE

GABRIELLE ZAPHON

THE ACORN PREROGATIVE

We never reflect whether the story we read be truth or fiction. If the painting be lively, and a tolerable picture of nature, we are thrown into a reverie, from which if we awaken it is the fault of the writer.

- Thomas Jefferson (August 3rd, 1771)

Bell Tower of Independence Hall - 520 Chestnut Street - Philadelphia, PA - Monday, December 26th, 2022 - 1:35 a.m.

With the return of an unblemished chicken egg, Gabrielle Zaphon knew it was safe to send a three-month-old baby 28 years into the past. She put away the jeweler's loupe, closed the lid on the Leyden jar and placed it on the metal floor of the time portal, an incidental invention Benjamin Franklin left in the bell tower of Independence Hall.

Gabrielle turned to Thad Vorax and said, "The egg made a successful round trip. Now hand me the boy."

Thad spoke into the tablet: "Video and heat signatures check out too, so there won't be a welcoming party when we arrived." He looked up with a scowl and said, "But I don't get it, Madame Zaphon. Three days ago, we shut the Confederates out of Port Wilmington. But today, we're kidnapping a baby and sending him to 1994?"

We don't have time for this, thought Gabrielle as she removed her straw hat, then adjusted her relaxed, lamb-white hair that was tied back into a sleek low bun.

"And another thing," Thad continued. "This portal has been here the whole time, and you never told the Regents about it?"

That was when Gabrielle noticed Thad's wrinkled shirt and knew something was wrong. He always wore neat, clean, and pressed clothes that complimented his tall frame and olive skin tone. But not tonight—the bright blue top and frayed jeans were anomalies.

Gabrielle said, "This portal is new, and it's not my decision to choose the time periods you protect or whom we move. Now, please dial in the year on the Leyden jar."

Thad entered the cage, and Gabrielle admired the craftsmanship of the forged iron sun that hung above the metal door. Its smiling face seemed to welcome anyone who entered America's first elevator that Ben Franklin designed, forged, and built in 1753. It looked like a giant birdcage and was tall enough to haul the carpenters, tools, and heavy equipment when the State House bell tower was under construction. It became obsolete after the final bell was installed, never to be used again for its intended purpose. That was, until Madame Zaphon recruited Croatian genius Nikola Tesla to calibrate the Leyden jar, which re-purposed Franklin's cage into a fully functioning time portal.

Thad picked up the Leyden jar and rolled the four numbers embedded in the gray graphene lid from 2022 to 1994, much like setting a combination lock on an old piece of luggage.

Gabrielle studied the sleeping boy as she placed him in a papyrus basket. The baby had shiny brown eyes and soft ringlets that swirled across his scalp like tiny hurricanes in a cocoa sea.

"When you arrive in 1994," said Gabrielle, "take him to Pennsylvania Hospital and leave him where he'll be found. Disable the cameras to make sure you're not seen, and—"

"First we abduct him, then orphan him," Thad interrupted. "And here's the trifecta: He'll be dead before he's thirty-three."

"This boy's lifespan isn't your concern. Nor is it mine," said Gabrielle.

Thad's time travel partner, Saimon Khnkhlạ̀ng entered the room and made his presence felt, despite his physical build and height of only five foot two.

"We don't question orders in the prerogative," said Saimon. "Remember what happened at Bull Run when you didn't follow them?"

Always the eager soldier, thought Gabrielle. Although his head barely reached Thad's shoulder, she knew Saimon was a fighter, be it physical or intellectual.

Towering behind Saimon was Michael Lokhem, an octogenarian like herself, and a close friend. Despite Michael's age, he kept the physique of Mr. Universe, which strained the sleeves of his green National Park Service uniform.

Thad said, "Why's Michael here?"

Gabrielle ignored the contempt in Thad's voice and replied, "Since the end of the Succession Prerogative, Mr. Lokhem has kept well-placed men and women in the United States Treasury Police, which has ensured our continued access to the South Wing portal. Now he's expanded into the National Park Service for protecting this one."

She approached Michael and greeted him warmly. Despite the war-toughened facade, she believed the big man might cry at any moment.

Michael said, "The perimeter is secure; no threats or anomalies."

"Madame Zaphon," said Thad, "why choose us for this one?"

Saimon rolled his eyes and said, "You know we're the only ones who can avoid a Wolfi-Pauli rip in 1994 because right now, in 2022, you won't be born for another couple years, and Madame Zaphon popped me out of the timeline in 1983, so I'm safe, too."

The first rule of time travel was the Wolfgang Pauli exclusion principle, a thing Gabrielle heard Regents call a "Wolfi-Pauli rip," which meant you couldn't travel to a destination year where you existed and see a double of yourself.

If you tried, you'd die—ripped from existence.

"Don't lecture me on death by time travel, Sai," said Thad.

"Then how about you stop arguing and follow orders," said Saimon.

Thad turned to Madame Zaphon and said, "Really, what kind of future are we saving him from? Will his parents' abuse him? Does he become a murderer? Why not send him to 1901? We have Regents watching over Tesla in New York City. They could take care of him—give him a shot at a full life. Or what about sending us to 2046, the day after you recruited me? It would be like I never left. I'd continue my law practice and raise this child in my future."

"Or maybe," said Saimon, "we save him from a future where he becomes a lawyer."

"You both know this baby's future is erased the moment he arrives in 1994, just like the first time you left." Gabrielle stopped and sighed. Now she was lecturing on time travel. "1901 isn't practical at all. Nikola requires constant monitoring on the Wardenclyffe Prerogative. I've already asked. Mr. Lamb assures me we're not saving this child from his parents or practicing law."

"Doesn't matter, Madame Zaphon," said Saimon. "What's the goal of this prerogative?"

"Once you get to 1994, both of you will watch over and protect this child, but from different perspectives. Saimon, you'll need to be in public, but invisible. And who's more ignored than the homeless? Keep close enough to watch over him and be ready to protect his life, even if it costs your own. Thad, your administrative, legal, and political skills are required because we need this boy to exist in the Philadelphia social services system, but not the state or federal systems. You'll place him with a caring foster family—"

Thad threw up his arms and interrupted. "A social worker? We just helped Lincoln preserve the Union. How's this anywhere near as important as—"

"We don't question orders!" Saimon shook the bars of the cage.

Gabrielle stood silently and took a deep breath before she said, "The War Between the States was a singular threat that required all Regents in the same time zone. But there's been a shift. This new set of prerogatives requires pairs dispersed across different times and places where new American anomalies have emerged. There's the Franklin Prerogative watching over this very tower in the early 21st during its restoration, and the Wardenclyffe Prerogative that's protecting Nikola in the 19th, especially after the laboratory fire that destroyed his life's work in 1895."

"What're the other ones?" Thad asked.

"The Founder's Prerogative has four Regents in 1775 assigned to cover the first American war for independence. The Montpelier Prerogative in 1812 has two Regents covering the second."

From inside the cage, Thad pushed his face up to the bars and said, "I'm up for another war."

Gabrielle thought Thad resembled the pathetic "In Jail" character on a Monopoly board as she told him, "You entered a sacred covenant when you joined the Regents. Do you intend to break it because you don't like the prerogative?"

"You know the consequences if you do," said Saimon.

Thad slumped his shoulders and stared at the floor for a long moment before saying, "I'd never breach a contract, even if I don't agree to it after it's been executed."

"Noted, Counselor," said Gabrielle. "This new prerogative may not be another war, but you never know. It could be dangerous in other ways."

Saimon entered the cage with the baby in the basket.

Michael then creaked the door shut and secured the latch.

Saimon said, "You never told us the name of this one."

Gabrielle said, "It's called the Acorn Prerogative."

Much like making French press coffee, Thad plunged the brass ball until it touched the lid of the Leyden jar, which activated the time portal.

Gabrielle felt Michael curl his powerful arm around her bony shoulder as she watched the departure.

The Leyden jar activated noisily and rose from the metal floor up to Saimon's hip. Then Thad, Saimon, and the baby basket rose three inches while snowflakes crawled across the bars of the cage. When the noise reached its loudest point, all contents of the cage disappeared with an icy flash of light.

The room went quiet, and the electricity shut down across the building.

When the backup power switched on, Gabrielle saw vapor rising from the crystals on the metal cage as quickly as they appeared.

Tears in her eyes, Gabrielle tilted her head to Michael as if peering at a tall building and said, "Displacing this baby was Mr. Lamb's last request. And now that he's gone, the Regents are his only guardians."

CHAPTER TWO

TOPHER WHITE

DARK WEB

Beware of those who speak of the spiral of history; they are preparing a boomerang. - Ralph Ellison (from *Invisible Man*, Prologue - published April 14th 1952)

Outside Fermi Nightclub - 4th & Kater Street - Philadelphia, PA - Tuesday, December 7th, 2010 - 1:35 a.m.

Before tonight, Christopher Franklin White didn't exist. He was a ghost in the machines across Philadelphia social services, a sixteen-year-old who cleansed himself from the computerized state and federal systems when he was nine. He went by "Topher" or "T" and lived off the grid in 2010, not out of paranoia, but preservation. Topher only used cash and never held a legal ID card. It was both independence and invisibility on his own terms, and he needed to keep it that way to protect himself. But now, as he faced two men he'd never met before, Topher didn't know that in his desperation to pay his foster brother's medical bills, he would unravel years it took to conceal his identity.

Topher pulled the sleeves of his blue hoodie over his wrists and glared at the short brown man lighting an unfiltered cigarette. The other guy, taller and whiter, stood next to the Smoking Man with crossed arms. *Big guy must be the brawn*, he thought.

"Kill the smoke or the deal's off." Topher couldn't hide his contempt for the habit.

Smoking Man took a long drag in reply, then slid the silver Zippo into his back pocket. Topher saw something clipped to his belt—a cell phone? Wearing a tan canvas coat, the Smoking Man looked more like a mechanic than a hacker. The white muscled guy next to him didn't appear the part either. He wore white-striped Adidas track pants and a gray peacoat. A red Manchester United Football Club logo appeared on his thigh, just below the jacket's hem.

Manchester slapped Smoking Man on the shoulder. "Oi, put it out! We got business to transact."

"Touch me again, I break your arm," said Smoking Man.

Manchester raised his palms. "Take it down a notch, mate."

Topher's first plan was to sell the five hundred credit card numbers on the dark web, but he needed a lot of cash quickly and didn't have the time to develop an airtight program that would conceal the digital trail those transactions would leave. For Topher, hacking was always about pushing the boundaries of what he could do—finding weaknesses in computer networks and programs deemed "unhackable." If he was being honest, it was mostly for the bragging rights. But not for theft or profit.

Until today.

Topher made an exception now because the money was for Todd, his foster brother, closest confidant, and protector. Nearly a month ago, Todd fought off three armed men to protect Topher, who did nothing but cower in the elevator. He didn't get a bruise, but Todd sustained a stab wound, broken elbow, and dislocated shoulder. Getting that fixed without insurance totaled fifty thousand dollars, and Topher had to make it right.

That was why he put this deal together. Topher couldn't pay Pennsylvania Hospital with stolen credit cards, and the buyers had agreed to pay in cash. But something seemed off with these guys, especially the Smoking Man. Was this some undercover thing, a trap? It wouldn't be the first time someone had tried to draw him out from the dark web IRL, but he had sought these buyers, not the other way around.

That greasy short man wouldn't stop smoking, so Topher pulled the left sleeve over his wrist and turned away.

"Okay, okay—hold up!" Smoking Man dropped and stomped the cigarette. "Let's go inside Fermi Club for this. Get you a drink. I know the bouncer—no ID needed."

"I don't mix booze n' business." Topher peeled the blue hoodie from his head, revealing an ashy forehead topped by a tangled Afro.

"How we know it's legitimate?" Smoking Man asked. "My boss is not forgiving, and if what you sell doesn't work, then—"

The delay annoyed Topher. "Hacked these myself. They're fresh, and nobody's better than me." Topher pulled his right sleeve over his wrist. "You got the cash?"

"Well, mate, fifty thousand ain't exactly pocket change," said Manchester.

"That's one Benjamin per number and they're worth half a mill, easy," said Topher. "Each number has 5K available, minimum. Some are as high as 10K. Free, easy credit to use how you want. Best part is, this transaction ain't traceable because it's vis-à-vis." Topher produced a matte black flash drive with a hand-drawn lightning bolt in silver Sharpie.

Smoking Man slowly ground the long-dead cigarette under his boot. "Thing is, we have forty. But to make it up, we know a guy with five new plasma TVs."

Counteroffers were normal, but Topher didn't like the price drop or offering things he didn't need and couldn't transport. Negotiations were always in chat windows, bulletin boards, and encrypted email — not like this. He'd breached credit card servers in the past, an exercise to keep his skills sharp. Life would've been easier if he'd gone the black hat route. But Topher earned his living from setting up and securing computer networks - cash only. It was safest, because he didn't want his lifestyle to arouse anyone's attention or suspicion.

As usual, the biggest problem wasn't technical; the data was solid. Getting past humans and receiving payment were always barriers.

"Does it look like I have a van," said Topher. "The deal was fifty, and these numbers'll get you 100 or 200K in the first four hours. That's until they make wise and lock youse out." Topher forced a fake smile.

"I have new proposition," said Smoking Man. "I know a guy in Chinatown. Has ten new Apple phones, the newest one. Sealed in the box. No van needed."

"Won't be in stores till next year–as in 2011, laddie," said Manchester.

Topher's eyes dilated involuntarily, and he said, "For real?"

There was lots of online hype about the upcoming iPhone 4. He did the math and knew it was a good counteroffer.

"I can get them in two hours," Smoking Man said. "We have deal?"

Topher pulled the right sleeve over his wrist and felt his stomach rumble. "I'll take the cash now. Phones later."

Manchester held out a hand. "Then give us the data stick."

Smoking Man tossed a heavy green backpack at Topher's feet. He opened it and quickly counted the cash—forty thousand. Topher handed Manchester the silver lightning bolt flash drive and said, "Deal." Topher slung the backpack over his shoulder with one hand and pulled the hood over his head with the other. "Meet you in two hours on 11th and Filbert near Jefferson Station."

Smoking Man and Manchester exchanged a smile as they walked away. Sometimes, Topher believed he could read faces almost as well as computer code. Maybe they thought they'd gotten away with something, so he shouted back, "Data's no good without the key!"

Smoking Man stopped and said, "We have a man who can get the data from this."

Manchester laughed. "Our guy's a hacker genius, fetus boy!"

"Then tell your genius this." Topher always got paid because he planned for safeguards. "I locked drive with a custom 768-bit cryptosystem, developed by yours truly. Stronger than what the US government or Israel uses. I doubt your hacker'll get in. But don't stress—you'll get the key after I get ten new iPhones."

Chapter Three

SAIMON KHNKHLÀNG

Jefferson Station

Associate yourself with Men of good Quality if you Esteem your own Reputation; for 'is better to be alone than in bad Company.
-Francis Hawkins (From the 1640 English translation of French Jesuit rules from 1595, an Inspiration for George Washington's work, *110 rules of Civility & Decent Behavior in Company and Conversation*

Outside Jefferson Station - N. 11th & Filbert Street - Philadelphia, PA - Tuesday, December 7th, 2010 - 4:00 a.m.

Jefferson Station at four in the morning was quiet, save for the horns and sirens floating above the hum of rolling tires. It was Saimon Khnkhlằng's lullaby and the best time to get some uninterrupted sleep, but not this morning.

An angry Brit tripped the city's rhythm.

"Our mate's better than anyone with a computer, and he can't unlock it, you git!"

Saimon moved the layers of cardboard sheets to see better. The Brit was large, maybe six-foot-two, with thinning black hair dyed blond. He wore Manchester United football pants and a buttoned-up peacoat.

The Brit continued, "Said something 'bout getting a key or prescription to get the data."

A much shorter man stood next to the Brit. "You think you can cheat us like that!" That accent was familiar too—Farsi? The Iranian pointed a Soviet-era Makarov PM at someone out of Saimon's sight-line. This was going to be a quick robbery or a messy firefight. He'd witnessed countless drug deals around Philadelphia, but this was about data. Computer nerds made deals online, not in person.

Something was weird about this, so Saimon slipped out of his makeshift bed to discover it was two against one. The soon-to-be victim wore a blue hoodie that covered his face and sagging jeans. The clothes told one story, but the body revealed another. Blue Hoodie pulled his right sleeve over his wrist, then switched and did the same to the left, a pattern that seemed stuck in muscle memory. Saimon also noticed Blue Hoodie's hands shook slightly.

The Iranian said, "You said you have a key. Give it."

Blue Hoodie pulled a key chain from his front pocket and held it out. "Only thing this key opens is my apartment. Where're the iPhones?"

Blue Hoodie had a North Philly accent. Couldn't tell if he was Black, White, or Latino. Teens in the early twenty-first took on the fashion, language, and attitude of hip hop culture, but skin tone didn't matter right now. He was caught up in a high-tech robbery on a low-lit street.

"Sure, whatever." Blue Hoodie tossed the key ring, and the Brit caught it.

The Iranian waved his gun at a nearby alley. "You must understand your place. Now we go to my office and talk manners."

The Brit poked a Webley revolver into Blue Hoodie's back and said, "Move it, you shite-headed muppet!"

Strange choice, thought Saimon. The Brit seemed more like a Glock 19 type, not an Indiana Jones wannabe.

Hands raised, Blue Hoodie said, "I wrote the encryption myself, so none of the keys your hacker genius has will work."

The Iranian gestured his gun to the backpack and laughed. "He brought money back!"

"Complete numpty, right, Finn?" said the Brit. "Nice of the lad to return it."

Finn... short for Phineas? That couldn't be the Iranian's name, Saimon thought as goosebumps erupted across his arms. Then he wondered if this was why Madame Zaphon sent him to this location every year.

The Iranian turned to the Brit and said, "One-eyed Jack won't like this, and neither will the boss. Let's use the boy's key."

Saimon thought, *Idiots. Do they really think a physical key will open a flash drive?*

The Brit shrugged his shoulders. Saimon knew he wouldn't decide, but unfortunately for Blue Hoodie, the Iranian pulled the hammer back on his gun. Saimon figured he'd shoot Blue Hoodie, take the cash, and keep the flash drive.

Job done.

Saimon remembered his orders while checking the magazine of his reliable Colt M1911: observe—don't interfere. He could just slip back into his urban bed and sleep it away. But this one had a different vibe from the start. Street disagreements were always over girls, money, or drugs (rarely in that order). Never a flash drive.

So, for the first time since becoming a time-traveling Regent, Saimon violated the rules.

He sized up the alley and inventoried assets: overhead pipes, dim lighting, and old bricks protruding from narrow walls. Saimon took several steps back, grabbed a nearby chunk of concrete, and sprinted at an angle. Once he reached the alley's entrance, he lobbed the decoy over their heads. Saimon then leaped to a loose brick jutting from the alley's right wall as the dumpster rang behind Blue Hoodie. That jolted everyone's attention long enough for Saimon to spring to the left wall, then to the right—back and forth like a pinball banging between bumpers until he propelled himself to the overhead pipe, about fifteen feet above ground level. There, he hung above the trio and waited for the right moment.

"Who's there?" the Iranian shouted.

The Brit moved toward the dumpster and said, "Probably some homeless sap."

"Last thing we need is a witness," said the Iranian.

Blue Hoodie continued to pull the sleeves over his wrists above his head.

Saimon watched the Brit walk behind the dumpster, about ten meters from the Iranian and Blue Hoodie.

"Nobody here," said the Brit as he holstered his revolver. "Probably a rat."

That was Saimon's cue. He released, did a flip-twist, and dropped to the ground between Blue Hoodie and the Iranian. Saimon swept a leg at the short man, tumbling him backward. When his elbow cracked on the brick-paved alley, the Makarov PM discharged. He cursed in Farsi as the firearm tumbled from his limp hand.

Saimon knew that bone-crunching sound too well.

He also knew Farsi.

A body fell to the ground behind him. Had the Iranian shot Blue Hoodie or the Brit? He swiveled and saw Brit approaching with a smile and a hand on his holster. The grin fell when Saimon drew his M1911 and took aim. The Brit stood above Blue Hoodie's body, but instead of freezing like most men would have in that situation, he drew the Webley.

Saimon heard metal scrape close behind him and believed that, despite the broken elbow, the Iranian must have been retrieving his gun. At this moment, he wished he had stayed in bed.

"Welcome to the party, shortie," said the Brit. "Now lower your weapon before anyone else gets shot."

Saimon remained crouched and raised his arms over his head, then lowered his gun hand.

"That's it," said the Brit. "Nice and slow."

Saimon set the M1911 on the alley floor and maintained close eye contact with the Brit.

The Brit shouted, "Finn, you okay, mate?"

In a pained-tinged voice, the Iranian said, "What you waiting for? Shoot him!"

Blue Hoodie convulsed with a loud, wet cough that sprayed blood onto the Brit's white shoes. The Brit looked down, flung out both arms in a questioning gesture, and said, "I just got these trainers, and now—"

Saimon snatched up his weapon, aimed, and squeezed off a perfect shot through the Brit's forearm, popping the Webley from his hand. It toppled to the paver, then twirled like a wobbly spinner on a warped board game.

Saimon spun around and faced the Iranian. Somehow, he'd gotten to his feet. He was also stupid enough to hold the Makarov PM with his non-dominant arm.

The Iranian tried to aim his weapon and groaned, "Stupid mother fuc—"

Saimon launched a forceful kick to the Iranian's ribs, knocking him back and dislodging the firearm from his hand. He then snatched up the Webley and took aim at the Brit while keeping the Iranian covered with the M1911.

A minute ago, it was two against one, but Saimon had flipped the ratio.

Saimon pulled the hammers back on both guns and said, "No one needs to die."

"You're a street bum, *khar*! A lucky shot!" The young Iranian clutched his elbow.

"Care to test your luck, *dostam*?" Saimon chose a kinder Farsi word.

"You mean to steal from us?" said the Iranian.

"You meant to kill him." Saimon nodded down at Blue Hoodie.

"I'm bleeding bad, Finn." The Brit seemed much smaller now.

"Take the money and leave," said Saimon, weapons trained on both injured men.

The Iranian yanked the backpack from Blue Hoodie's twisted arm. He then swore at the much paler Brit who was clutching his blood-soaked peacoat. Saimon traced their sluggish exit with both guns until they were out of sight.

His attention then went to Blue Hoodie, who struggled to breathe. Saimon holstered his weapon and went into field-medic mode. He placed a hand on Blue Hoodie's chest. Blood, thick like warm syrup, covered his fingers. This teenager would bleed out and die if he didn't call an ambulance, so he opened his Razr flip phone and tapped a text to Madame Zaphon: send AMB @ my 20.

Saimon pulled the hoodie back to see if the boy was conscious. His face was familiar, but his eyes were closed. The shape of his ears triggered a faint memory, but he pushed it back. This kid needed real medical help, not a soldier. He pulled Blue Hoodie's sleeve back to check his pulse and couldn't believe what he saw. Countless small and large circular scars spread across his inner arm. Some were flat. Many were puffed up keloids. They didn't look recent, and he knew exactly the cause: cigarettes and cigars, not self-inflicted. They looked five to ten years old. Some sadistic prick had burned Blue Hoodie's inner arm when he was a child. He looked closer and saw a small parting in the middle of the forearm among the scar clusters. A straight, one-inch surgical scar.

It couldn't be.

How?

Saimon's mind raced, and his chest tightened. The age of the teenager, the shade of melanin, and mid-arm surgical scar put it all together. Had Thad cut out the tracking device? Did he torture and burn the child's inner arms, a child under his care and protection? Or did it happen after they disappeared? Through tear-filled eyes, he sent another text: STAT—AMB 4 ACORN!

T he ambulance arrived, and Madame Zaphon swung the doors open. Her appearance startled Saimon. She tilted her head and said, "Do I detect tears?"

"Of happiness, Madame." Saimon rarely showed emotion, much less talked about it. He understood loss from his days with Army Special Forces in the early '80s, but losing Christopher White under his watch all those years ago had been different. Now that the child, now a teenager, had been found, another idea occurred to him. What if his choice to disobey orders was predestined, something planned to happen in a cosmic, pre-written script? Had Madame Zaphon known Christopher would be here tonight? There was no way Saimon could have known the teen in the blue hoodie was the same child he had lost years ago, so he sighed the idea away.

If there was a puppeteer, it was a cruel play.

Madame Zaphon said, "You must leave before the police arrive." She offered Saimon a handkerchief as the paramedic, Jimmy Truebody, arrived with an unconscious Christopher strapped to the gurney.

"Assessment, please," said Madame Zaphon.

"Gunshot wound to the chest. Definitely a collapsed a lung."

"Will he survive?"

Jimmy guided the gurney into the ambulance as he said, "Needs a hospital, Madame Z. I ain't got a chest tube, and he needs it."

"It's him. It's really him," Saimon whispered. "He was selling a data stick to a Brit and an Iranian."

"International business at four in the morning?"

"Problem is, one of 'em looked like a Broker from the Succession Prerogative, only younger. Much younger."

"Did you run the facial recognition algorithm?"

"All the Brokers are supposed to be dead."

"Did you confirm it was Christopher in the alley before you rescued him?"

"Is this why you send me to Philly every December?"

"Don't answer my question with a question."

"Apologies, Madame. Didn't FRA anyone—didn't have time."

"Then why did you get involved?"

"Had a feeling."

"You don't do feelings, Saimon. Tell me what really happened."

"I woke to an argument about credit card data and encryption keys. The Iranian got real mad and was about to kill him. Would've died if I didn't intervene. The young Brit called the Iranian Finn..."

Saimon swore in Thai at the improbable realization that the two men were at the same time traveling Brokers from his previous Prerogative during the Civil War.

"Language," said Madame Zaphon. "Now, did you get the name of the British man?"

"Sounded like he was from Manchester–and I'm pretty sure it's Corbin Raum if I could have confirmed the Iranian as Phineas Ophis." Saimon produced the revolver. "Corbin left this antique behind—a Webley. Bet we could get prints off it. I've never shot one of these."

"Put that weapon away." She pushed at Saimon's hand. "Too bad you couldn't run Matija's facial recognition algorithm to confirm your theory."

"Why don't you call it an FRA like the other Regents?"

She didn't seem to hear the correction, but stared past Saimon and said, "Now this is the definition of irony."

"What do you mean?"

"You find Christopher over the theft and sale of other people's identities?"

"It was credit card numbers," said Saimon.

She continued: "Yet all these years we couldn't find him because he hid his identity so well." Her eyes, blue as the waters of the Belize Barrier Reef, filled with tears. "I'll ride along and see him to the hospital."

Saimon said, "I hurt The Brit and Iranian. Won't be too hard to track them down and run an FRA to be sure it's not Phineas and Corbin —"

"You're done for tonight. Get to the safe house."

"But what if—"

"Go now. An eye scan or FRA will get you in."

Saimon left before the flickering blue and red police lights started their dance across the alley's walls.

Chapter Four

GABRIELLE ZAPHON

The Betrayal

The cause of America is in a great measure the cause of all mankind. - Thomas Paine (January 10th, 1776)

Prinus Ambulance En Route to Pennsylvania Hospital - Philadelphia, PA - Tuesday, December 7th, 2010 - 4:40 a .m.

Gabrielle Zaphon removed her white straw hat before entering the back of the ambulance.

She watched Christopher's chest rise and fall with a disturbing gurgle and pushed back the pain of how Thad betrayed the Regents and this child.

Jimmy cut the patient's sleeve to prepare an IV and cursed. Gabrielle didn't approve of swearing, especially taking God's name in vain. She glared at him, then became more unsettled at the sight of Christopher's arm.

She stuttered, "These aren't new."

Jimmy wiped his forehead and sighed. "My granddaddy had puffed up scars like these. Told me he got them putting up barbed wire. Every cut turned to keloids."

"Fencing didn't cause these," said Gabrielle.

Gabrielle didn't know if the abuse happened before or after Christopher and Thad disappeared seven years ago, and now she wanted to know who inflicted the torture.

The investigation produced two leads that explained Thad's vanishing, but raised more unanswered questions. The first was a Swiss bank account in the name of James Ticarios, an alias Thad had used throughout the Succession Prerogative. It was opened seven days before he left, and it had a thirty million Euro deposit, but no withdrawals. The second lead was from the last place anyone suspected: security footage from the United States Treasury Building's South Wing. That was the location of the second time portal the Regents built after the first was compromised at Fort Sumter. The video revealed Thad and another person entering the secret passage to that time portal. Thad set the Leyden jar to 1865, which led to a Wolfi-Pauli rip.

Suicide by time travel.

More shocking than Thad's death were the FRA results of his time-traveling companion in the South Wing portal. She was one of the Count's henchmen, Astra Barakel, a Greek astronomer who had seduced and manipulated men on both the Confederate and Union sides. Gabrielle could only conclude that Thad sold out the Regents for thirty million euros to reveal the location of their time portal.

The biggest unanswered question was whether Thad did it to protect Christopher or if they paid to abandon him.

Besides the tracking chip found at the bottom of the Schuylkill River, Madame Zaphon and her team of 12 Regents couldn't find the 9-year-old child. From the start of the Acorn Prerogative, Gabrielle had insisted on keeping duplicate foster records from social services. She sent Saimon to visit the address of every foster family to whom Christopher had been assigned from the time he was an infant, left at the steps of Pennsylvania Hospital until his disappearance. But there was nobody left to interview—every foster parent was dead or had disappeared without a trace like Amelia Earhart, Glenn Miller, or D. B. Cooper.

Although Christopher seemed to have evaporated from existence, Gabrielle believed he was still alive. That was why she sent Saimon to Philadelphia every year around the anniversary of when he went missing.

Gabrielle watched Jimmy slide an IV needle into Christopher's hand and secure it with tape. She felt a mix of relief and sadness.

Jimmy said, "That'll do for now."

Christopher's eyes opened wide. He reached for his wrist, then tugged at the tube in his hand.

"Yo, yo, yo, don't pull that!" Jimmy eased Christopher's hand. "You've been shot. My name's Jimmy. I'm taking care of you."

Gabrielle heard someone arrive at the back of the ambulance. It was an officer by the name of Bledsoe who spoke into his notepad. "Victim have a name?" When his eyes met hers, the police officer flinched. "Oh, Madame Zaphon, didn't see you there."

Christopher's voice redirected Gabrielle's attention when he wheezed, "Zuse . . . Konrad . . . Zuse."

She played along. "Like the Greek god Zeus?"

Morphine slurred Christopher's speech. "No . . . Z-u-s-e."

"Officer Bledsoe, you'll have to question Mr. Zuse later. He requires immediate medical attention."

The old cop sighed, snapped shut the notepad, and closed the double doors.

When the sirens wound up and the ambulance was on its way, Gabrielle looked into Christopher's eyes and said, "My name is Gabrielle Zaphon. People call me Madame Zaphon. I own the Prinus Ambulance Company. The ride is on me today."

Christopher only stared in reply.

She continued. "It took years to build this ambulance company and my other ventures. But they aren't my greatest achievements. My real life's work is to help the youth of Philadelphia. I use my time and resources to help those who've chosen a life of self-destruction. Too many young men your age get caught up with gangs and selling illegal . . . things."

"Excuse me, Madame Z. I need to check something," said Jimmy.

"He's lucky." She watched Jimmy secure the bandages. "A gunshot wound to the chest is usually fatal."

"Got that right," said Jimmy.

She felt shaky. "Today, young man, it's a blessing you're alive."

He blinked in response, but it didn't matter. She had to voice her thoughts. "There's been a miracle. And despite the pain you're feeling, this could be an opportunity. A time to choose a different path. Leave this gang life and get an education. If you improve yourself, then, in turn, you'll improve Philadelphia."

"What you talking about, Madame Z? Just because he wearing saggy jeans don't mean he's in a gang." Jimmy shot an antibiotic into the IV line. "Just got himself in a tough spot. That's all."

"Perhaps."

"Besides, he don't hear you now—unconscious."

"I can play a role in this young man's life, no matter how large or small." She sighed. "Jimmy, whatever this young man becomes, even if he fails, he's my fate."

"Madame Z, due respect and all, but I think no sleep's got you talking crazy. What's this he's your fate about? You're going on and on over him, and I tell you, this kid ain't a gangbanger."

"How do you know?"

"Name's Konrad? I mean, for real?"

"And?"

"Sorry, he might wear the costume, but he don't look like a gangsta, and I seen plenty."

"I'm sure you have."

"Just because he's young and Black doesn't mean he's in a gang."

"Mr. Truebody, you're right." Gabrielle felt embarrassed for being so openly dramatic. "I am deprived of sleep and don't take ride-alongs as much as I used to."

"I'm not saying you're old."

She put a hand on Jimmy's shoulder. "And I shouldn't make assumptions."

"Nobody should."

"I am very interested to hear Mr. Zuse's story when he becomes conscious."

CHAPTER FIVE

REX PURSON

THE BROKERS OF GIOVANNI ROSSO

Après moi, le déluge. (Translation: After us, the deluge.) -Attributed to Jeanne Antoinette Poisson (a.k.a Madame de Pompadour) (November, 1757)

Giovanni Rosso's Office - 40 Wall Street, 74th Floor - New York, NY - Tuesday, December 7th, 2010 - 9:00 a.m.

Rex Purson was violently disappointed with Phineas and Corbin. As the first recruits into his new, specialized group called the Brokers, they were failures. Getting a flash drive from an unarmed teenager was supposed to be easy, but no, some homeless guy fell from the sky and wrecked the job. If this wasn't a video conference, Rex would've aggravated their injuries personally.

"We got the flash drive, mate," Corbin pleaded. "Jack's still trying to open it."

"Kept the cash, too—nothing lost," said Finn.

His one word response to their ineptitude was "*Arschgeigen!*"

Rex killed the conference call, then approached the mirror to regain composure. Within forty seconds, Rex's cheeks transitioned from red to his natural gray complexion.

He adjusted his gray silk tie and told his reflection, "Speaking of ass-fiddlers, now I have to tell the boss what happened."

Feeling more poised, Rex grabbed the handle of his walking stick and strolled the mahogany-lined hallway to Giovanni Rosso's office. A violin behind the doors grew louder while Schoenberg's "Concerto" spilled under the doors of the 74th floor penthouse office. He mumbled, "The man has enough money for a thousand lifetimes. How will stolen credit cards alter the America's future?"

Rex burst the doors open and shouted over the performance, "*Entschuldigung Sie bitte! Herr Rosso!*"

Giovanni faced the window and gave a virtuoso performance to his captive audience below on Wall Street. Despite the music's intensity, his thick black hair didn't move. For a man in his mid-forties, especially for one who rarely exercised, Rex thought he was surprisingly fit. Giovanni wore a tailored white shirt and a silk magenta bow tie that peeked above the cloth wrapped around the violin's lower bout.

Rex sank into the brown leather couch to endure the last movement.

When Giovanni finished, there was a dramatic pause for inaudible applause. He then carefully interred the priceless 1738 Guarneri del Gesù into its carbon fiber case and turned to Rex. "*Bitte benutzen Sie Englisch*, Rex. And you only use *Sie* with me when something's wrong."

Rex evaded the accusation and replied, "Phineas and Corbin got the data you requested, Herr Rosso."

"Very good."

"And your German is passable, even for a *spitzpinkler*." Rex enjoyed insulting Giovanni's middle-aged, metrosexual lack of manliness. Toilet jokes were his favorite.

"And?"

Rex felt the blood rising to his cheeks again. "Herr, they—"

Giovanni smiled. "You're blushing. I haven't seen you this red since you found me shagging Madame de Pompadour."

Rex managed a smile and willed his normal gray complexion to slither back. Giovanni loved to boast of how he charmed the most beautiful woman in France, a claim few men could make.

Rex grabbed a Waterford tumbler from the bar and pointed at Giovanni. "The king believed that the child you sired was his own. And I spared you from the gallows. Of course, that little tryst spoiled your long-term scheme with Herr Voltaire."

"Reinette was so very, very lovely." Giovanni rolled his sleeves down and fastened the French cuffs. "What's got you so rattled?"

"We have the credit card data, but it's locked on a flash drive. Jack tried to release it—said it's encrypted better than the Israelis, like nothing he's ever seen."

Giovanni scoffed. "I'm not impressed. Isn't Jack was one of your elite cyber soldiers?"

"We agreed to call them Brokers, not soldiers." Rex jabbed a text into his Motorola Droid, tossed it on the bar and continued: "Why steal credit card numbers, anyway? It's a low reward to risk ratio. *Kinderspiel.*"

"It's not for me; it's for Jack. He wants to fund some cause. You know how he is—saving the environment, the polar bears, or whatever's the fashion."

"I fail to see how saving the environment will take down America, Herr Rosso."

"This venture isn't about making money. It's a recruiting exercise, one that could meet our mutual long-term goal and fulfill your obligations to me."

It was tiring how Giovanni always used that same line before any big ask.

"I'm listening," said Rex.

"If Jack can't unlock the data from that stick, then we need a better locksmith. Maybe flip this mishap into an opportunity." Giovanni pulled a bottle of rare Mendis coconut brandy from his desk and presented it to Rex. "Does this Philadelphia hacker have a name?"

Rex could only stare at the unicorn on the bottle of rare spirits.

"An identity?" Giovanni removed the cap and waved it under his nose. "Perhaps another hacker could join these Brokers. We'll need that level of talent for what I have in mind."

Rex didn't want to reveal that Phineas had shot the Philadelphia hacker. He also didn't want to explain how a homeless guy nearly blew off Corbin's lower arm. No, he'd tell his boss after a drink from that million-dollar brandy.

After consuming nearly half the bottle, Rex slurred, "In nearly nineteen years, you're no closer to collapsing the United States of America before everything gets worse. I've seen how bad it gets in the future. It's where I came from. You're from a time when electricity was just a theory."

Giovanni said, "We've had success in steering the past. Killing Kennedy and putting Johnson in charge was effective."

"That was the twentieth. Bad things happen in the early twenty-first, in a little over six years from now, the year 2016. This stealing of credit card numbers will be no more effective than blasting Jack's brains on Jackie's face. I propose we adopt more aggressive tactics."

"High risk, high reward? I'm listening."

Rex removed a weapon from his shoulder holster and plopped it on Giovanni's desk. "This is a photon-charged revolver from my time in the late twenty-first. Brokers Astra and Marquis will take four to 1775 through our time cage in Germany."

"For what purpose?"

"First, they sail to Philadelphia, which will have them arriving in spring of 1776."

"You've got the year wrong. George Washington doesn't become president until the spring of 1789."

"By the summer of '76, they already declared independence from Great Britain."

"I've been in America long enough to know that. Get to your proposal."

"I say we kill the men responsible for the Declaration of Independence."

"Sounds like a shortcut."

Rex cracked a snake-like smile and said, "It will stop America before it even begins."

CHAPTER SIX

TOPHER WHITE

THE ESCAPE

Pennsylvania Hospital - 800 Spruce Street - Philadelphia, PA - Friday, December 17th, 2010 - 1:05 p.m.

Topher woke from a wandering sleep with red-hot coals in his ribcage; every inhale blew them hotter. His throat felt like someone had cleaned it out with a wire brush. When he tried to say something, only air emerged; he couldn't talk. A computer with blinking lights attached to a vertical tube told him where he was, but he couldn't remember how or when he arrived. When the embers in his chest were most unbearable, the machine beeped, his mind went fuzzy, and the fire extinguished.

The next time the pain jolted him back to consciousness, Topher spied a lab-coated doctor entering the room, followed by a man wearing an ill-fitting trench coat with frayed red lining.

He closed his eyes and faked sleep.

"We removed the breathing tube this morning," said the doctor, who sounded female. "It's a good sign he doesn't need a ventilator."

"Now that the thing's out of his gob, Doctor, can I talk to him?" Trench Coat had an accent.

"He's had four broken ribs, a collapsed lung, and a damaged pulmonary artery. Lucky to be alive, Detective Capaldi."

"Aye, but can he gab a wee bit?"

"Gab?"

"Talk. Can the lad talk, Dr. Crenshaw?"

"He's been in and out of consciousness and has a very sore throat. It can wait."

"I don't think I can wait. There was fresh blood at the crime scene that didn't match your patient. How do I explain that without a witness?"

"Gabrielle Zaphon is covering security at the hospital. She even put a guard at the door for Mr. Zuse, although I don't see the sense in it."

"How's that relevant to my investigation?"

"He's effectively a prisoner here." Topher felt the doctor lift his left arm. She had icy hands. "This may not be the worst he's been through."

It was hard for Topher to keep up the act because the flare in his chest ignited.

"Okey dokey. I'll be back in a few days." Detective Capaldi left the room.

Dr. Crenshaw gently set Topher's arm on the bed.

The machine beeped, and a drug-induced sleep replaced the burning in his chest.

T odd's voice brought him back. "Hey, little guy, you're safe now."

Topher wasn't in the hospital anymore. He looked down and saw he was wearing silver and blue pajamas. His chest no longer ached, but fresh injuries on his arm caused him to pull up his left sleeve to see why. Covering his inner arm was a constellation of cigarette and cigar burns. Near his elbow was a line of fresh stitches that parted the round, throbbing wounds.

Todd wiped tears from his eyes. "They messed you up real bad, T. Sorry I couldn't be there. Could've stopped 'em if I knew they did that to you."

"It's not your fault."

Why's my voice sound so high? Topher wondered.

"Mr. Vorax saved you from them—brought you here."

"My social worker?"

"Yeah. He acted real scared. Told me it was my turn to keep you safe because I've aged out."

Topher pointed at the scabs on his right forearm. "From Lion-man?"

"I don't know. Now listen," said Todd. "Mr. Vorax gave me a fist full of cash before he bounced. Said it'll help."

"The police can do that."

"No, they won't, T. Mr. Vorax said you need to disappear—can't never be in the systems."

"Systems?"

"That computer stuff you do. He said they'll find you if you don't stay out of 'em. Kept saying that over and over."

"He burned me, Todd. Screamed questions I didn't understand. Put out cigarettes on me if I didn't answer."

"Mr. Vorax?"

"No. Lion-man."

"You know how to get out of those systems he's talking about?"

"I need a computer and a phone line."

"You got it."

"And some cookies."

The next time Topher opened his eyes, he was back in the hospital bed. The pain from that drug-induced memory moved from his inner arm back to his ribs; it felt like ropes tightening around his chest. The Teen Titans Cyborg pajamas he loved as a child were now loose green pants and a shirt with sleeves too short to pull over his wrists.

Blinking lights refocused Topher's attention; they appeared above a small green screen with pixelated numbers—a simple computer attached to a pole. Liquid-filled bags with clear tubes running in and out of it hung on hooks above the computer. That box must have been the nexus controlling the painkillers. If he could reduce the flow of drugs without the doctors or nurses knowing, then Topher believed he could stay awake long enough to devise an escape plan.

He stared at the interface, but did not know how to access the operating system controlling the flow of drugs. Topher White could breach the most secure computers in the country undetected, but he didn't know where to start with this one.

Frustrating.

He noticed that the tube stuck to the top of his hand went into the plastic box with the computer. *Maybe I'm making this too complicated*, he thought. Topher then wondered how he was getting rid of the liquids from the bags hanging from the vertical tube. He reached below the sheets and found a much larger tube taking liquids out of his body. He couldn't leave with that attached; a clear bag of pee might get noticed.

Molten marrow seemed to fill his ribs when he rolled to the other side of the bed. The pain blurred his vision, but when it came into focus, he saw a keyboard and a monitor on a cart just a few feet away. Now, that was a familiar interface. But when he tried to reach it, the beep dragged him away from consciousness.

When he opened his eyes, Topher got an adrenaline surge because a gun's barrel was inches from his face. He took a few steps back and noticed he wasn't in the hospital shirt anymore. This time, he wore a black, long-sleeved compression shirt, and he was back at the underground poker game with Todd.

Topher looked beyond the gunman and saw Todd holding a cognac snifter. He threw it at a brick wall to draw attention and yelled, "Hey, what you playing at?"

The shattering sound pierced Topher's eardrums like a high-pitched fire alarm.

The man with the gun yelled, "He's hiding cards! Ain't no way you got a royal flush." He pulled Topher's sleeve back and swore.

Todd reached around and snatched the man's gun away with a quick twist and a loud crack.

The big man screamed as his broken finger flopped above the top of his hand.

It shouldn't bend backward like that, thought Topher as Todd pulled him away.

"Youse just chill now." Todd pointed the gun at the broken-fingered man as new men in gray suits emerged with more guns. It was hard to hear what they said because everyone across the makeshift poker lounge grabbed their winnings and scrambled away.

Full panic mode.

Todd shouted in Topher's ear, "Stay behind me, and you move only when I move! Got it?"

The broken-fingered man lunged toward them, but Todd responded with a rapid jab to his throat, punching his Adam's apple.

Topher couldn't see the guy's reaction because Todd was dragging him into a nearby birdcage elevator. The ascent was dizzying, and it felt like someone punched him in the ribs. Maybe the face, too—his nose must have been bleeding. Fear rose in his chest so strongly that all he could do was ball up in the elevator's corner and listen to his heart beat faster.

The bell rang on the top floor.

Three bulky men in gray suits waited behind the sliding metal door.

One had brass knuckles.

Topher tried to yell, but no sound emerged. He clenched his eyes and opened them, only to see the green blinking light that kept sending him back to repeat past traumas.

All at once, he realized it was the thugs in gray suits who put Todd in the hospital. That was weeks ago. Topher blinked hard and remembered that someone in an alley shot him while trying to sell credit card numbers, all to pay off his foster brother's medical bills.

Topher believed this situation was some bizarre twist of fate humor, but couldn't think of a word to describe it.

A new song from The Roots came to mind about not being old enough to know he was on his own gave him despair. Todd couldn't rescue him this time.

Topher used the bed's control to sit upright and reach for the keypad on the box attached to the pole, but hesitated before pressing any buttons. He looked at the top of his hand and realized a non-technical solution might work, but he was running out of time. The burning in his chest got worse with each breath, bringing him closer to another drug-induced nightmare.

Sitting upright was unbearable, so he reclined and gently removed the tube from the top of his hand before the machine beeped. Sure enough, the box must have been delivering the drugs. After a few seconds, he put the tube back, and the pain went from a boil to a simmer. That small dose gave some relief. If it was a full one, that would knock him out again, sending Topher back to repeat terrible memories.

Once he reeled that hospital terminal on a cart to his bed, it was time to work.

Topher's multi-phased hack would cover medical records, phones, security cameras, and fire protection. Good thing Pennsylvania Hospital had old systems—many weaknesses to exploit. Several lines of reliable code stored on his encrypted cloud drive sealed the cyber phase. The work would take at least four beep cycles, but he was fast and efficient despite the pain, which somehow kept him sharp.

Priority was erasing any evidence he was ever there. Topher found all the records, including photographs, X-rays, surgical notes, and test results under his alias, Konrad Zuse. The most disturbing was the number of inner arm pictures; why did they have to take them? He also deleted all off-site back-up records and covered his tracks on the hospital's system to ensure it had scrubbed all the data.

The biggest data problem wasn't electronic. Never was. There were always paper records. He remembered the nurse with the clipboard. Mentally, he noted he would need to grab that on the way out.

Pulling the tube from his pud was next. His first instinct was to yank it out, but an Internet search on male catheter removal changed his mind quickly. If he didn't deflate the balloon before pulling it out, the pain would be worse than the broken ribs and be a lot more embarrassing.

With the plastic third leg extension gone, Topher could leave the bed.

Now that he could move, albeit slowly, it was time to get people moving. He looked at the phone and figured he'd call Todd for a physical assist on this escape plan, but rejected the idea because he was still recovering from his own injuries.

Topher White was on his own.

He went back to the keyboard and entered the first set of commands that disabled the voice-over IP phone system and overrode the security cameras. That way, any call to the police or the fire department wouldn't get out, and they wouldn't record his departure.

The next command triggered the fire alarm on the opposite end of the building. That would draw first responders away so Topher could leave undetected.

He checked the security camera at the nurse's station and saw a muscular security guard barking orders in Spanish above the sirens. It was the same guy who guarded the door, which was good—the ruse had drawn him away. Topher knew the fire department would be there soon because he couldn't disable cellular networks, but he also couldn't exit the room until the nurse's station was clear. Destroying the paper file was just as important as purging the electronic records.

They weren't clearing out fast enough, so Topher triggered fire alarms across the entire complex. He heard distant sirens approach at the other end of the hospital. His planned route would be clear. Through the window of his door, Topher saw the nurse's station was finally empty. He took a deep breath, stood, and opened it. Head peeking into the hallway, he saw the main elevator and a traffic jam of wheelchairs and gurneys to the left. Muscle-Guard was helping the geriatric patients, but Topher knew he'd soon come back.

He looked to the right and saw the service elevator: freedom.

He pushed the door open with his right arm and entered the hallway, then hobbled to the nurse's station and found the "Konrad Zuse" file - right on top, easy to find.

He stuffed the file under his right arm and walked to the maintenance elevator. A sluggishness crept into his legs with each step; the competition between his brain, body, and lungs left him hobbling.

Topher also had a strange feeling he was being watched, so he turned back and saw Muscle-Guard standing at the end of the hallway, legs spread apart with a cell phone clipped at his hip like it was a holster packing a six-shooter. He was also a lot shorter than he appeared on the camera feed, but swole.

They stood at opposite sides like a Wild West shootout at high noon. Over the blaring sirens and blinking lights, Muscle-Guard yelled, "Zuse! Evacuation's this way, genius!"

Topher felt deflated—the plan was a failure.

Human factors always messed up a good hack. Muscle-Guard unholstered the phone and flipped it open. Was he calling for backup? No, not with alarms and evacuation in progress. Anyway, the Philadelphia police and fire departments would be there in less than a minute. Even if he got into the service elevator, they might catch him outside. How would he explain the hospital gown and medical file under his arm?

With heavy legs, Topher shuffled backward.

He didn't break eye contact as he watched the Muscle-Guard flip the phone shut and re-holster it.

The blinking lights and sirens had a dizzying effect, and the ache in his ribcage was warming again. These bodybuilder types were strong but not fast, right? With that logic, Topher pivoted away and made a run for it. When he took the first stride, it was like running through a pool of warm Jell-O. The red button on the service elevator was his only focus, but with each step, it was as if the gelatinous fluid rose above his waist, then to his chest, and finally his eyeballs because everything went blurry.

Then there were no bad dreams.

Only darkness.

CHAPTER SEVEN

TOPHER WHITE

A BETTER PHILADELPHIA

Penn Mutual Building - 510 Walnut Street - Philadelphia, PA - Friday, December 17th, 2010 - 11:04 p.m.

Topher White didn't feel like much of a genius when he found himself back in a hospital bed. The world outside a ten-foot window had a view of Independence Hall below, imparting a sense of fear and dread. He was in an office, not a patient room. Just behind him, guarding the wooden door, was that muscled-up security guard; name on the Quercus Security tag read Juan Trueno.

The escape plan had failed. Topher wondered if this was some sort of holding area before getting turned over to the police. He lifted his arm and noticed he wasn't handcuffed or strapped down like a hospital prisoner on TV.

The door popped open, and an old woman entered, which startled Topher. She wore a white pantsuit and over-sized white hat like the ones you'd see at an Easter egg hunt. Doesn't she know it's Christmas time?

"See," she said to Juan. "It took no time at all." The woman hung the bonnet on the door's hook and stared at Topher. Her eyes were dark, almost navy blue—had to be colored contacts. He'd never seen an old black lady with eyes that shade.

She pulled a thick paper file from a leather bag, thunked it on the desk, and paused dramatically between names: "Christopher . . . Franklin . . . White."

Topher jerked his hand to the left side of his chest and felt blood seeping through the green hospital gown.

Thick with sarcasm, she said, "And I thought your name was Konrad Zuse." She picked the file up and handed it to Topher. "Go ahead, open it."

He couldn't believe there were any paper records left; Topher had spent years infiltrating the Philadelphia social services. With help from his foster brother, Todd, (and some well-placed bribes), he'd been able to confiscate all documentation of his existence. This had to be some ruse, and Topher was going to call this thin old granny's bluff.

"Who are you?" Topher said with a rasp, realizing this was the first time he'd spoken since being shot.

"I'm Gabrielle Zaphon. I own Quercus Security, Prinus Ambulance, and Durata Janitorial. We've met before, but you were bleeding and unconscious."

Topher's heart jumped to his throat when he opened the file and found duplicates of the hospital records he knew he had deleted. Underneath, the data went much deeper. There was complete documentation of every foster home he'd ever occupied. Topher and Todd had stolen and destroyed those records years ago. How could an old black lady and a muscled rent-a-cop threaten the invisibility he'd established and fought to maintain for nearly nine years?

Topher said in a near whisper, "What's this about?"

Juan said, "The police will be very interested to know we've found you alive. Right, Madame Zaphon?"

She raised a hand. "No, Juan, *por favor*. Get Mr. White some cold water. He appears dehydrated. And fetch Cordelia. It seems our patient has broken sutures."

"*Sí*, Madame." Topher noticed he said it respectfully.

Topher flipped the folder shut after Juan left. "Okay, so you have friends in the police, the hospital, and social services. But there's nothing electronic to back this up. It's probably a forgery, Mrs. Zaphon."

"I never married."

"Say what?"

"I'm not a missus because I never married, and I'm far too old for miss; therefore, I prefer madame."

"So, why are you here?"

"You did an excellent job purging your existence. Off the grid for years, and from such a very young age. You have a gift."

Topher's chest burned, and he wondered, What's this Madame Zaphon playing at? Is this punishment for nearly escaping the hospital? He didn't know, but he also didn't want to satisfy her with a frightened reaction.

With the smallest dose of emotion, Topher said, "What's your point?"

"I rode with you in the ambulance that night. You see, Christopher—"

"It's Topher. Don't call me that."

"Topher, I'd like you to know the profits from my businesses aren't only for my benefit."

"If you're here to make me pay the ambulance bill, I won't have cash until—"

She interrupted. "You misunderstand. Money is a tool that can be used for good or for evil. Those profits allow me to do good work—to help the people of Philadelphia."

Topher cleared his sore throat. "I don't follow, Madame Zaphon. How's showing me this file helping Philadelphia?"

Juan burst into the room and handed Topher a cold bottle of Evian. A short, curly-haired brunette with a medical bag followed. Madame Zaphon motioned for Juan to sit, and he complied. The brunette opened the bag and removed some vials and instruments.

Madame Zaphon's dark blue eyes teared up, and she said, "But I can help you."

"How?"

"Because money itself won't make you happy. In fact, the pursuit of money only yields temporary happiness."

Topher took a sip of water. It cooled his throat before saying, "Says the woman with money."

"Tonight, I give you a choice."

"How about I choose to leave here right now?"

"I don't believe you're in any condition to do that," said Madame Zaphon. "It's more of an offer than a choice."

"Which is?"

"If you agree to get a high school diploma, I'll give you a perfectly legal job with Durata Janitorial, which will help maintain your independence."

"I can't go back to that hospital."

She nodded to the brunette and said, "Cordelia is a brilliant physician and will attend to your recovery, starting right now."

Dr. Cordelia gave Topher a shot, and the pain in his chest subsided.

With an effort, Topher proposed, "How about I skip high school and go straight for a GED?'

Going back to school would be a bore for Topher, and taking a job as a janitor wasn't the problem. What bothered him was how she got the information, and why?

"And when you have a high school diploma or the equivalent, a GED, I'll shred these files in your presence. I'm offering a new start."

Topher took another long swig of Evian. It felt good. "Wait, having a legitimate job means I have to use a legal name, and I ghosted myself years ago."

"What if your legal name becomes Topher Franklin White? Then Christopher Franklin White can stay off the grid and remain a ghost, if you will."

He hadn't expected that. This Madame Zaphon seemed the law-and-order type, but was she really suggesting a new identity? He felt cold scissors at his chest. Dr. Cordelia efficiently cut away a flap of the hospital gown with a blue-gloved hand. She then dabbed the blood oozing from the surgical cut on his left side before giving a series of small shots around the broken stitches. The medicine provided relief and didn't cloud his mind.

Topher said, "Let's just say that's possible. First off, let's drop the 'Franklin' from my ghost name. But then this new 'Topher White' would need a legal birth certificate, a social security number, school records, address history, etcetera. Look, I'm good at erasing identities, stealing them even. Creating them IRL—how'd you even begin to—"

Juan interrupted. "Matija Bogadan could do it without breaking a sweat. Right, Madame Zaphon?"

"Who's Matija?" Topher looked at Juan; he seemed less angry.

"She'll create your new legal identity," said Madame Zaphon. "But you'll have to do the actual work."

"I'd like to talk to this Matija - know if she has the chops to do this."

Madame Zaphon got out her iPhone and put it on speakerphone. After drilling Matija for nearly 30 minutes on every aspect of creating a new identity both electronically and logistically, it convinced him she had both the skills and experience to do it right.

Madame Zaphon looked out the large window throughout the conversation. When it ended, she said, "Durata Janitorial will have an opening for the night shift at Independence Hall for a Topher White who will pass all required background checks."

Topher looked past her, saw it was 11:04 on the clock tower of Independence Hall. He knew he could forge a new state identity, and the birth certificate would be tricky, but not impossible after what he learned from the call with Matija. He could then hack some fresh credit card numbers and sell them on the dark web to pay off this Madame Zaphon to get the paper records.

Topher asked, "How much for the files?"

"I'm not interested in earthly wealth. I have enough of that."

"What you want then?"

"A better Philadelphia."

Topher felt tugging on his chest, but no pain. He looked down and saw Dr. Cordelia tying off a knot at the end of seven new stitches.

"Okay, I'll play. How do I get those files back?"

"First, get yourself healed and start your new job. During that time, you must study and prepare for the GED exam. That's compulsory. And absolutely no illegal hacking on the side."

"And if I don't agree, this file goes to the police and social services, right? Sounds like blackmail or extortion."

"I'm offering you a fresh start with a new name and a legitimate job with a paycheck."

"What's your point?"

"It's only extortion if you're forced to do something illegal."

CHAPTER EIGHT

BENJAMIN FRANKLIN

CITY OF BROTHERLY LOVE

In 200 years will people remember us as traitors or heroes? That is the question we must ask. - Benjamin Franklin (March 16th, 1775)

Port of Philadelphia - First Street - Philadelphia, PA - Friday, May 5th, 1775 - 9:00 a.m.

B en Franklin watched the city bob into view as the ship approached the Port of Philadelphia.

New buildings and churches rose across the skyline, but it looked like competing cities waving back and forth. He shook his head, squinted, and opened his eyes. That familiar burning rose to his throat, and he couldn't stop it this time. Ben lurched his head over the rail and hurled a dark stream of red into the Delaware River.

Was that blood? He wondered.

"The Bordeaux you requested, Grandfather."

Ben wiped the vomit from his lips and turned to Temple, his fifteen-year-old grandson.

"Thank you."

"That's the last. Barrel's empty."

"We've been on this ship for six weeks." Ben snatched the pewter goblet from Temple's hand, and it splashed onto the deck. "How could it run out?"

"I tapped it Wednesday and you've only allowed me one cup."

Ben sighed and said, "City of Brotherly Love, but I fear there's little love left for me."

"Please sit down. You look pale."

Temple guided Ben to a nearby chair as the boat glided past Windmill Island.

"Do you know why I spent all that time in London?"

Temple rolled his eyes. "To petition the king. You've told me this."

"No, the real reason." Ben tipped his head back, gulped the wine, and belched.

Temple didn't reply.

"Because I am a loser."

"What?"

"I mean, I lost my seat on the Pennsylvania Provincial Assembly back in '64. You were a young lad then."

"That was a long time ago."

"It was that article I wrote years before you were even born. I criticized those German immigrants for hanging on to their culture, and you know what those Quakers did?"

"No."

"They called me intolerant. Said I hated anyone who wasn't English!" Ben saw his cup was empty. "Another drink, Temple."

"But the Bordeaux is gone. How about some breakfast? Tea, perhaps?"

"I'm done with those micks, sheep shaggers, and tea baggers! The lot of them can all go to—"

"Why are you so agitated, Grandfather? We've almost docked."

"First, I'm not going home when I get off this ship. They're probably waiting to arrest me for being King George's spy . . . and thirdly, my cup is dry."

"That was two things. Here, have the rest of my cider."

"Pour it in there, good boy." The hard cider was sweet against Ben's palate as he thought, *This will be my last drink as a free man.*

"Can we get breakfast after we deboard?"

"Do you know why we're back in Philadelphia?"

Temple sighed. "They wanted to arrest you in London over those letters you sent."

"I could have been a hero, a peacemaker."

"They put you through the mill, Grandfather."

Ben stumbled when the boat bumped into the dock. "I was naïve, boy."

Temple took Ben's arm. "Let me help you off the ship."

The alcohol dulled the pain in his knee, but it wobbled as Temple helped Ben down the creaking plank that led to the pier.

An old man's cheerful greeting disrupted Ben's self-pity. "Welcome home, Dr. Franklin."

Ben dipped his chin and peered above his small oval glasses. "Thank you, sir." *Here to take me into custody*, he thought. The greeter had a rolled newspaper under his arm. "Is that today's paper?"

"Yes, Dr. Franklin. It's for you." He held out an arm. "You're lacking your land legs. Can I help you?"

"He's in his altitudes," said Temple.

"Forgive me, sir. Do I know you?"

"No, you wouldn't. I'm Jim Timios, a volunteer in the Pennsylvania militia. Mr. Hancock sent me."

He's definitely the constable, Ben thought. "Aren't you a bit long in the tooth for the militia, Mr. Timios?"

"Once a soldier, always a soldier."

"Fought in the Seven Years' War, did you?"

"I've fought in many wars, Dr. Franklin. Please, call me Jim."

"I assume the meeting is with Hancock Jr." Ben felt dizzy as the acid hit his throat. He took Jim's arm and thought, *Better not flash the hash on the constable.*

"He's at City Tavern with a Samuel Adams." Jim smiled, then added, "And his cousin, John Adams."

"No need for the newspaper if Sam's here."

"You look like you could use a strong cup of tea, Dr. Franklin."

"The tea can stay in England. As long as I am in America, I shall drink coffee."

The bells suddenly rang at the nearby Christ Church and it startled Ben. Other churches joined in for several long minutes.

"It's not Sunday," Ben shouted.

Jim smiled and spoke, but Ben couldn't hear what he said.

"Is there a fire?" Ben said after the bells stopped ringing.

"No, Dr. Franklin. They're to celebrate your arrival. Welcome to the City of Brotherly Love."

After a disorienting carriage ride, Ben received strong black coffee at City Tavern, not handcuffs. They had a light breakfast and when the small talk fizzled, an uncomfortable silence hung over the table.

"If it weren't for Mr. Timios over there," said John Hancock, "the lobsterbacks would have put us in shackles."

Sam Adams said, "They would've given me a lead enema, and weren't there to arrest us, John; it was to kill us and the Cause!"

John Adams, Sam's cousin, pounded his fist on the table and said, "It means only one thing: all-out war with Great Britain."

Despite the third glass of wine, John Hancock seemed tense. "Dr. Franklin, do you know if the British planned these attacks on Lexington and Concord?"

Ben finished his coffee and waved for another. "Of course not, Mr. Hancock. But I tell you this, if I'd stayed any longer, they would have locked me up in the Tower of London, bound in chains!"

Mr. Hancock winced at the jest while Sam and John managed a smile. Perhaps it was the caffeine sobering him up, but Ben's self-pity faded.

"The timing of your arrival is perfect, Dr. Franklin," said Mr. Hancock.

"I doubt that." Ben sighed. "By my calculations, I'm six months too late."

"I was very sorry to hear of Debora's passing," said Sam.

"I should have taken passage last fall." Ben felt tears forming. "Instead of coming home to my sick wife, I wrote that God-forsaken proposal."

"Dr. Franklin, reconciliation's no longer possible," said John Adams. "Yet there are still some hold-outs in the Pennsylvania delegation blood soaks the fields of Lexington and Concord."

"Quakers," Ben scoffed. "All they want is peace at any cost."

"We need your voice," Mr. Hancock pleaded. "We need you in the Continental Congress. Tomorrow, new delegates are being selected for another session. Who could decline Dr. Franklin?"

"My knee hurts, Mr. Hancock. Weeks at sea have inflamed my gout."

"Dr. Franklin, please call me John. I'll reserve the most comfortable seat in the State House for you. But tomorrow, all you need to do is show up for delegate selection."

"You'll be a sight for sore eyes," said John. "The triumphant return of Dr. Franklin!"

"Meetings start five days after that," said Sam. "You can rest before things start."

Ben wiped a tear from his eye. "Perhaps the timing of my arrival isn't as poor as I feel it is."

CHAPTER NINE

JIM TIMIOS

CRIMSON SPLENDOR

It is courage, courage, courage, that raises the blood of life to crimson splendor. Live brave-ly and present a brave front to adversity! -
Horace

City Tavern - 138 S. 2nd Street - Philadelphia, PA - Tuesday, June 11th, 1776 - 10:30 p.m.

Until tonight, it had been three uneventful months since Ben Franklin's arrival and appointment to the second Continental Congress. Madame Zaphon warned of an imminent threat to Ben Franklin and the other four members of the committee of five, and Jim Timios wanted to know more details. Of course, she told Jim it was "need to know." In his experience as an OSS agent during World War II, that phrase meant one of two things: either they did not know what was coming or the danger was worse than one could imagine. His background in espionage served him well as one of the time-traveling Regents, and regardless of where and when he went, information was always currency. But at this moment, Jim felt bankrupt in his assignment called the Founder's Prerogative.

He turned to the window facing 2nd Street in Philadelphia and touched the latch of his pocket watch, activating the cochlear comm to talk to his partner, Cordelia. "Anything on the scan?"

"Only period locals and livestock near the State House," said Cordelia, the youngest of the Regents who gave up a surgical residency at Johns Hopkins during the 2015 riots to become a time traveler.

"Let's hope the threat isn't bovine," said Jim, trying to keep the mood light and mask how nervous he felt.

"This heat's making my boobs sweat. When's that rain coming?"

"It'll happen. Has Z ever been wrong?"

"Never on the facts, at least the ones she cares to reveal."

"Yeah, and I'd rather know imminent's schedule."

"The threat can't be the Brokers; they died in the 1860s."

Jim sighed.

"What is it?" Cordelia asked.

"Adams is raging again."

"Have fun with that."

Jim clicked the watch shut and pivoted to the founders under his and Cordelia's protection: Benjamin Franklin, Roger Sherman, John Adams, Robert R. Livingston, and Thomas Jefferson. Earlier this afternoon, the 2nd Continental Congress formed a committee to write the Declaration of Independence. What did they do after receiving such an important historical task? Go to City Tavern and get drunk.

With a slight slur, Adams spoke as if delivering arguments to a jury. "Gentlemen, June the 11th will be recorded as a momentous day in the annals of history. We are on the path to independence, free from the tyranny of King George the Third."

Robert R. Livingston, the twenty-nine-year-old New Yorker, said, "It'll be an act of treason. We'll hang from a rope, every one of us."

Franklin quipped, "I've never been fond of twine cravats—too itchy at the neck."

Adams continued: "Today's stall tactic will delay the vote for another month, and for what reason, to form yet another committee to draft a declaration? John *Dick*inson's obstruction shall not stop the inevitable." Jim thought it funny how Adams emphasized the 'dick' part of the surname. "We'd save the Continental Congress a lot of time if we gave them a copy of Common Sense. I swear, Dickinson must be the only literate person in the colonies who hasn't read it!"

Franklin spoke into his Madeira glass: "I assure you he has John. Mr. Dickinson doesn't see independence as the only option because he's a pacifist. It runs thick in his Quaker blood."

Adams pointed accusingly at Livingston and said, "Everyone knows what the Regulars did in Boston and Charleston. And what about the buildup of ships around Manhattan Island? There are reports of white sails and Union Jacks as far as the eye can see."

Jefferson, the thirty-three-year-old redhead, interjected. "King George the Third is using the military to show the colonies he's in control."

John flung his arms wide dramatically and said, "The British Navy has the firepower to flatten every building on that island before dinnertime. Goodbye, York City."

Livingston quietly asked, "How can words on parchment stop an armada?"

"The pen is the tongue of the mind," said Ben. "Thomas Paine's pamphlet courageously articulated exactly how many colonists feel."

"And everyone thought you wrote it, Dr. Franklin," said Adams.

Roger Sherman, the fifty-five-year-old Connecticut lawyer, clinked his teacup onto the saucer and belched delicately. He was the only one on the committee who refused alcohol.

In a low, squeaky voice, Jefferson said, "It is courage, courage, courage, that raises the blood of life to crimson splendor. Live bravely and—"

"—present a brave front to adversity." Sherman finished the quote.

"That's right, Roger," said Adams. "The courage of General Washington and the Continental Army will rise up and defend our imminent independence!"

A long, uncomfortable silence followed.

"Horace," said Sherman.

"Excuse me?" asked Adams.

"The quote is from Horace, a Roman poet."

Jefferson said, "Mr. Adams, I feel you misunderstand its meaning."

Adams said, "Enlighten me, Virginian."

Jefferson's cheeks turned as red as his hair.

Sherman explained. "Mr. Adams, I believe it means that when we face adversity, even a British armada, we should be dutiful and brave. With courage, this committee shall carry our appointed task and steadfastly write the Declaration of Independence."

Lightning crashed outside, followed by a legato thumping of raindrops that quickly rose to an adagio drum roll above their heads. When the rain reached its crescendo, Cordelia burst into the room and approached Jim's table. Jim smiled and thought, *She almost passes as a young man in that uniform.*

She held out two soaked envelopes and whispered to Jim, "A messenger gave me these at my post."

The first one had the red wax seal of John Hancock. The second envelope had a jade green wax imprint of a Madonna lily, which was unmistakably from Madame Zaphon.

"What's her directive?" Jim asked.

"Extraction—now," said Cordelia.

"I haven't picked up anything on my scans," said Jim, and his pocket watch buzzed. He flipped it open, and the hairs on his arms stood at attention at what he saw. Cordelia leaned over and probably came to the same conclusion: The threat had arrived, and it wasn't from this time. The watch showed two individuals on the Delaware River. Both had late twenty-first-century weapons—photon-charged revolvers and were en route to City Tavern.

"I'll take this one," said Cordelia to Jim. She then approached the table with Franklin and the other four and addressed them: "I'm Thaddeus Begeistert, New York militia. Mr. Hancock requests this committee's immediate presence at the State House."

Adams said, "I believe John Dickinson's up to something."

Franklin broke John Hancock's seal from the letter and said, "What could be so urgent?"

"He said to make haste. Dr. Franklin," said Cordelia as she extended her hand, "allow me to help you."

Franklin waved it away, read the letter, and said, "Mr. Timios will assist if necessary, young man."

"What is it?" asked Adams.

Franklin said, "It seems Mr. Hancock has some urgent instructions regarding the declaration. And we must depart after I've finished this drink." He drained the Madeira and belched loudly before saying, "Okay, Jim. I am ready."

The rain slowed the transport on the carriage ride to the State House. Jim hoped that would also slow the others with the non-period tech. With advanced weaponry like that, he assumed they intended to murder the men under his and Cordelia's protection. It wasn't the first time this had happened. During his first assignment, called the Succession Prerogative, Jim and Cordelia foiled or stopped multiple assassination attempts on Lincoln and his allies. That was until J. W. Booth used that Derringer to kill the president. Jim surveyed the area for threats through enhanced spectacles that looked like Franklin's; the software showed no anomalies on the north side facing Chestnut Street.

Jim hurried the five men through the Central Hall to the Tower Stair Hall at the back of the building and they made the ascent.

Cordelia whispered over the comm, "Proximity alert. Those two are coming in hot—photons lit up and ready."

Jim whispered back, "Are they close enough for an FRA?"

"Yes—processing," said Cordelia.

Cordelia cursed through the comm.

"Who's coming?"

"You read Madame Zaphon's letter. Get them into the time cage, Jim. Now!" She said in a panic, "How're they still alive?"

"Tell me who we're facing," said Jim.

"It's Astra and Marquis," said Cordelia.

"They're supposed to be dead."

"Last time we collided, that shrew Astra nearly cut off my ear!"

CHAPTER TEN

JIM TIMIOS

THE FRANKLIN CAGE

I know not what course others may take; but as for me, Give Me Liberty or Give Me Death! - Patrick Henry (March 23, 1775)

Independence Hall - 520 Chestnut Street - Philadelphia - PA - Tuesday, June 11th, 1776 - 10:55 p.m.

As he led the grumbling committee members up the creaking stairs into the bell tower room, Jim's heart tightened at the thought of sending five Founding Fathers to the year 2011 at *exactly* 11:04

p.m. *Why'd Madame Zaphon specify that year and time?* He wondered.

Jim said to the caretaker, "Mr. McNair, I'm putting them into the elevator."

"I don't take your meaning," said McNair, caretaker for the Pennsylvania State House. "Here is your egg from the Leyden jar."

Jim took it and inspected it with a jeweler's loupe. He couldn't believe Madame Zaphon would suggest using the time portal to secure the founders. There were only two threats, and Jim was ready to join Cordelia and stop them, a much better alternative to displacing historically important people.

Jim pointed at Franklin's Bell Lift Cage and said, "Everyone - in there—it's the safest place if lightning strikes."

Looming in the northwest corner was a ten-foot tall, ornately wrought iron cage. The Leyden jar that enabled time travel was its only occupant.

Franklin said, "The State House has lightning rods. We're safe anywhere in this building because I installed them personally."

Jim removed the Leyden jar from the cage, dialed it to 2011, then said to McNair, "Quick—get downstairs and barricade the doors. Nobody enters this building!"

Adams demanded, "What's going on here, exactly? Mr. Hancock summoned us. Why the urgency? And why up here?"

Jim said, "Remember this, Dr. Franklin?" He then helped each one into Franklin's Bell Lift cage as he monitored his pocket watch, which just turned 23:02.

Once inside, the founders were understandably bewildered.

Adams spit, "Do you mean to imprison us? Are you a British spy?"

Jim placed the Leyden jar at their feet, closed the cage door and said, "Please, for your protection, you must remain inside Dr. Franklin's invention."

Jefferson placed his hand on Adam's shoulder and said, "It's only a storm."

Jim said, "I'm here to save your lives, Mr. Adams. And I'm an American spy."

Jim Timios had learned the craft of espionage as a young man during World War II as an agent in the Office of Strategic Services. It became the Central Intelligence Agency after the war, which he served in until 1967. That's when Madame Zaphon found him at age sixty-one in Thailand to recruit him as the oldest and most experienced member of the Regents.

Franklin stared at the Leyden jar near his ankles. "What's that, Jim?"

"You of all people should know, Dr. Franklin. It's a Leyden jar, and it's going to save you from who may break down the doors any minute now."

Livingston asked, "Who's breaking down the doors?"

Jefferson said, "Are we under attack?"

"It must be the British!" shouted Adams.

Head bowed, Roger Sherman prayed.

Jim really hoped Cordelia would fend off their old enemies so he wouldn't have to depress that brass knob on the Leyden jar.

Jim jumped when he heard the gunshots through the drumming rain, followed by a flash of lightning. It was less than a minute before he had to depress the plunger on the Leyden jar for the larger strike. He shouted downstairs, "Mr. McNair! Andrew! Andrew!"

It was in vain. The storm was too loud.

Jim said over the comm, "Cordelia?"

Nothing.

Ten seconds now; he had to go.

Jim heard a single set of footsteps running up the stairs, but didn't have time to see who was approaching.

He had no choice.

He depressed the brass ball on the Leyden jar like he was making French press coffee and closed the iron door. At exactly 23:04, a burst of light filled the circular windows of the bell tower. In the wake of the lightning strike, the Leyden jar on the floor hummed loudly and rose as high as Ben Franklin's hip, but not for long. All five founders elevated about three inches and their heads nearly touched the cage's domed roof. Snowflakes crawled across the cage.

A silhouette appeared at the door.

Jim unholstered his weapon and took aim. "Hands up—identify yourself!"

Behind him, the noise of the Leyden jar reached its loudest, and a frigid flash of light filled the room. Jim's only concern was, Who will be there to receive them in 2011?

CHAPTER ELEVEN

CORDELIA BEGEISTERT

THE PARIS SADIST AND ATHENS MINX

Into whatsoever houses I enter, I will enter to help the sick, and I will abstain from all intentional wrong-doing and harm, especially from abusing the bodies of man or woman, bond or free. -Excerpt from the Hippocratic Oath (1923 Loeb edition, English translation)

Independence Hall - 520 Chestnut Street - Philadelphia, PA - Tuesday, June 11th, 1776 - 11:02 p.m.

On the Walnut Street Side of Independence Hall, Cordelia Begeistert tracked the approaching anomalies beaming from her Swiss pocket watch. The hologram showed them twenty-five meters out and armed, two guns each—all photon-charged revolvers. *This is Philadelphia, not Tombstone*, thought Cordelia. The FRA identified the threats as Brokers named Marquis Amon and Astra Barakel, but the Regents called that duo the Paris Sadist and Athens Minx.

How were they still alive?

Madame Zaphon had said this might be dangerous, but she hadn't said it would involve their time-traveling enemies from the Succession Prerogative. The goal of that five-year assignment had been to help Lincoln preserve the Union. And Cordelia, along with the other eleven Regents, had prevailed; they stopped the Count and killed eleven of his twelve minions. But the deceased sadist and minx were now approaching fast, so she took cover to make sure they wouldn't see her.

Cordelia thought, *What if they're here to kill America's founders? That way, the Civil War and Abraham Lincoln wouldn't have happened.*

Now wasn't the time for paradoxical questions. It was 11:02. She had to hold them off, otherwise the orders were to activate the Leyden Jar at *exactly*

11:04 p.m. If Jim and Cordelia faced them together, they'd stand a chance at defeating the Brokers and not having to use the portal at all.

Cordelia tapped her watch and said, "Jim, they're at the tower doors and I'm gonna stop them. But if I can't, we'll have to do it Madame Zaphon's way and push the plunger."

No reply.

"Jim?"

Cordelia was short, only five-feet-one with raven-dark, curly hair and a gymnast's build. But she had a black belt in Krav Maga, a deadly form of martial arts she had mastered while in medical school at Duke University. Her hand-held Puckle gun was no match for their weaponry, so she'd have to get in close to disarm them.

She peeked around the corner and saw that Andrew McNair had opened the door. Even through the rain, she could see the fright in McNair's face because Marquis was pointing a revolver at his chest. Marquis pulled the trigger, which emitted a purple burst of light that toppled McNair straight back into a puddle like a domino.

Cordelia tossed off the tricorn hat, let her hair down, ran towards Marquis and Astra, and shrieked in a panic-stricken voice when she was right behind them: "My heavens, is he hurt? Shall I call for the doctor?"

Both spun around with surprised looks.

Marquis pointed the gun inches from Cordelia's face and spit, "None of your business, woman!"

Cordelia quickly pivoted her body out of the line of fire, grabbed the weapon, and twisted it from Marquis' hand. The gun flashed above their heads as the bones in his index finger snapped. She followed that move with a hard kick to the groin, which flopped Marquis into the puddle next to Andrew McNair. She backed several steps away as Astra unholstered her gun, but it was too late. Cordelia had already drawn her hand-held Puckle gun.

Before Astra could raise her weapon, Cordelia shot her in the chest three times. It was without remorse. She remembered how Astra had raped her fellow Regents, the Vaderlander twins at Fort Sumter, in the spring of 1861, which was followed by days of torture at the hands of Marquis. That was in the early days of the Succession Prerogative. The Paris Sadist and Athens Minx left them with permanent psychological and physical scars. Pulling the trigger was more than self-defense; it was revenge.

Cordelia then turned her gun on Marquis, who was pain-ridden but conscious. She activated the hologram on her Swiss watch. No new threats, but what if more Brokers of the Count were out of range? The sky suddenly lit up like flashes from a hundred cameras on the red carpet. After what felt like several minutes, her eyes refocused on the puddle. Only Andrew McNair remained. She checked his pulse to verify if he was dead. Luckily, he had been stunned, not murdered.

Cordelia slipped into the Tower Stair Hall and started a scan. The Brokers were in retreat on Spruce and 6th Street. She tapped the watch and said, "Jim, abort."

No response.

"Jim, can you hear me? They're on the run," said Cordelia.

It was 11:03, with 30 more seconds to go. If she ran fast enough, she could stop Jim from activating the time portal. She bounded up the first set of stairs. At the top step, she felt a tug at her thigh and braced her fall on the first landing with her forearms. Her gun tumbled forward and hit the wall. Cordelia looked back and saw the leather strap that held the holster to her thigh had come undone and gotten caught in the banister.

She cursed and shouted into the comm, "Don't send them. I'm coming to you!"

There was no response as Cordelia grabbed her weapon and headed up the next flight of stairs.

"Jim?"

Nothing.

It turned 11:04 when she entered the level two bell tower just as lightning shone through the circular windows. For the second time that night, the sudden brightness disoriented Cordelia. In the wake, her eyes refocused on the northwest corner to see it was too late. The Leyden jar was already humming loudly as it rose from the metal floor, followed by the levitation of five Founders inside. At nearly six feet, three inches, Thomas Jefferson's head nearly touched the top of the domed iron ceiling.

Cordelia stepped forward and must have cast a shadow because Jim spun around, unholstered his weapon, and took aim.

Both hands were on his Browning Hi-Power.

Even if Cordelia had screamed her loudest, Jim wouldn't have heard her above the noise of the Leyden jar.

The room went quiet and vapors trailed from the crystals on the portal's bars as quickly as they had appeared.

"Great job. McNair is down and we have the Paris Sadist and Athens Minx on the loose in 1776 with photon-charged revolvers."

Jim lowered his weapon. "And I just sent five Founding Fathers to 2011."

CHAPTER TWELVE

TOPHER WHITE

AN INVESTMENT IN KNOWLEDGE

[A] great Empire, like a great Cake, is most easily diminished at the Edges. - Benjamin Franklin, from Rules By Which A Great Empire May Be Reduced To A Small One in The Public Advertiser (September 11, 1773).

Independence Hall 520 Chestnut Street - Philadelphia, PA - Saturday, June 11th, 2011 - 11:04 p.m.

Although Topher White had a photographic memory, he pulled the letter from his locker during the break from janitorial work at Independence Hall. He wanted to make sure it matched the image in his mind. The score from the GED exam was a perfect 4000, a reward that validated nearly five months of studying at the 7th Street library. With proof he passed that stupid high school equivalency test, Topher knew his contract with Madame Zaphon was fulfilled and his time with Durata Janitorial would finally end.

Now that he'd held up his end of the deal, that crazy old woman would have to relinquish the files and photos she held for ransom. Topher planned to shred that evidence of Christopher Franklin White's identity and move on without fear.

Working the graveyard shift inside a national landmark wasn't that bad; the hardest part was staying awake, so he filled his body with a double espresso and occupied his mind with the building's history. Studying the Declaration of Independence and the Constitutional Convention for the GED was one thing, but cleaning the same rooms where one was signed and the other happened was another. It felt more real to see it, not just read about it. There was only one place he wasn't allowed to go: the bell tower. It was going through an expensive restoration inside and out since 2010. He heard rumors about an old birdcage elevator Benjamin Franklin built up there decades before the Declaration of Independence, and Topher was curious to see if it was real.

Growing up in Philadelphia, you couldn't escape old Ben Franklin. Topher didn't understand why that man's face and name permeated Philadelphia, especially around Center City. So the guy flew a kite and did electrical experiments; was that the reason for all the statues, plaques, and portraits?

He stuffed the test score letter into his backpack and remembered the vocabulary word he linked to Franklin: polymath. Topher made that association because when he studied (the only time he'd ever opened a history book on purpose), he learned Franklin did more than that kite experiment. He published newspapers and wrote books called almanacs. The electric battery, bifocal glasses, and stove were all invented by him. He mapped the Gulf Stream on the Atlantic Coast and invented a system of government called the Albany Plan. The best part was that Benjamin Franklin did it all without going to college or being born into money. Everything he accomplished was through hard work and a brilliant brain. And he did it his way. Knowing that, Topher had to give props to the fat old white guy in the roadkill hat.

Topher was about to text the GED news to his foster brother Todd when he heard a low hum from upstairs. His iPhone showed 98 percent battery at 11:04 when the sound quickly merged into a rumble. He checked the environmental controls on the wall. Something was wrong. One section on the second floor near the bell tower construction entrance read negative 15 degrees Fahrenheit, but it was a normal 70 across the rest of that level. Must have been a faulty control because of the renovations.

The noise suddenly wound up like a jet engine speeding across a runway, and it shook the building. Was this an earthquake? When it reached its loudest, the power went out across the building.

Dead silence.

No electricity or alarms.

The backup lights flickered to life within ten seconds. Topher checked his mobile and noticed the battery was 5 percent at 11:05. *Weird*, he thought. He grabbed a flashlight to check out the bell tower on level two. Topher knew he wasn't allowed there, but no one from the National Park Service had arrived yet, which was also strange. They'd come soon enough, and his curiosity compelled Topher to learn why the thermostat was off. Once he made the ascent around the stairs surrounding the Tower Stair Hall, the first stop was the bell tower's entrance.

Before he got there, Topher heard thudding steps coming from behind him. He turned and saw it was Juan Trueno in his Quercus Security uniform—the same Juan who had caught him six months ago while escaping Pennsylvania Hospital, trapping him into this job.

Juan caught up and said, "Power's out for the entire block, *esé*. Buildings, traffic lights, everything."

Topher pointed the flashlight in Juan's face. He wasn't supposed to be there, yet there the muscle head was out of breath and sweating.

"Yeah, blown transformer or something," said Topher. "Why're you here?"

"Madame Z's orders."

"When did she call you? Power just went out. Besides, the—"

"Was on my way, so you get the rest of the night off." Juan moved past the yellow construction ribbons and reached for the door.

Topher put his hand on Juan's forearm and said, "I work for Madame Zaphon, not you. Besides, I've got something to show her. Wait here while I get it."

Topher hopped down the stairs to get the GED letter from his backpack and wondered why Quercus Security was first on the scene after a blackout. Where were the Park Service rangers in the green uniforms, the ones who did the *actual* security at Independence Hall?

He sprinted back up with the paper and couldn't find Juan in the hallway.

Topher shouted through the bell tower door, "Where'd you go?"

"Go home!" Juan said from inside. "Madame Z can wait!"

Topher held the ticket that would free him from this job, and someone had to see it. So he climbed the creaky wooden stairs and found the room more meat locker than bell tower. Melting snowflakes covered the construction equipment and every metal surface. In the northwest corner was a cage that looked like an elevator. Icicles dripped from its domed roof. The iron bars glimmered under the dim lights. Franklin's hidden invention, Topher realized.

Something definitely had gone wrong in here. Had an air conditioner compressor exploded? More shocking than the ice were the occupants. Several dazed men in colonial costumes were crowded inside like clowns in a Mini Cooper. Juan struggled to creak the door open. After he flung it wide, he spun around and had a look like he'd just been caught taking steroids.

"*¡Hijo de puta, Cristóbal!* What're you . . ." Juan stared at Topher for a long moment, then turned to the shivering men who appeared unable to move.

Topher held up the paper and said, "I wanted to show you this, but what are those guys doing in there?"

Juan stuttered, "Seems . . . these actors . . . wandered into a construction zone."

They swayed a bit and seemed unsteady as Juan helped them exit the birdcage elevator. The decoration above it was a metal image of the sun's face that dripped tears from its eyes. The oldest of the group was last and looked like he was about to pass out. Juan showed him to a nearby toolbox and sat him down.

The old guy said to Juan, "I've not made your acquaintance."

"I'm an *amigo*, a friend," Juan said with a gentleness Topher had never heard.

"A Spanish Quaker?" The old guy rubbed his knee.

Topher felt disgusted when he realized what these men were doing up here. He got close to Juan and said, "Are they drunk?"

"*Sí—exactamente*," said Juan.

"How'd they get up here?"

"Madame Z's gonna write me up if the Park Service finds out." Juan picked up a glass jar from the cage's metal floor.

"I'm done with her and this job after she sees I crushed it on the GED exam." Topher waved the paper at Juan. "Besides, it's not your fault these actors got themselves locked up in here. Let the feds in green handle it."

Juan jabbed an aggressive finger at Topher. "No. You're going to help me get them out of the building before they arrive, so *vaminos*."

"Is that what they were drinking?" Topher pointed his flashlight at the glass jar under Juan's arm. It had a ball in the middle of the lid.

The old man in the chair placed a hand on Topher's arm and said wearily, "There was a lightning storm."

"Something knocked out the electricity," Topher said as he folded the test results.

The old man asked, "What is on that paper in your hand?"

"Scores from a test I took that are gonna get me outta this job."

"I always say an investment in knowledge pays the best interest."

"Sounds like something Ben Franklin would say."

The old man looked at Topher with penetrating, gray eyes and said, "That's because I am Benjamin Franklin."

CHAPTER THIRTEEN

TOPHER WHITE

A MAN FULL OF TROUBLE

I do not mean to say that the scenes of the Revolution are now or ever will be entirely forgotten, but that, like everything else, they must fade upon the memory of the world, and grow more and more dim by the lapse of time. In history, we hope, they will be read of, and recounted, so long as the Bible shall be read...

- Abraham Lincoln (January 27, 1838)
From: *The Perpetuation of Our Political Institutions: Address Before the Young Men's Lyceum* delivered in Springfield, Illinois

Independence Hall - 520 Chestnut Street - Philadelphia, PA - Saturday, June 11th, 2011 - 11:10 p.m.

Topher had seen plenty of men play the part of Benjamin Franklin, but this one was easily the most convincing. He didn't wear a cheap white wig but had natural, long gray hair that hung to his shoulders and a severely receding hairline. The clothing didn't look store-bought, either. His black shoes had thick heels and large metal buckles unlike anything he'd ever seen the other actors wear around Central City.

The smell was more authentic than the attire. Topher sensed alcohol the minute he got near the birdcage elevator, but when he helped the old actor to his feet, Topher gagged involuntarily, realizing this drunken Franklin hadn't showered or used deodorant.

Juan said, "Get him walking now. I'll help the others down the tower staircase."

"He's got a bum knee," said Topher. "After all that drinking, I'm surprised any of them can walk."

The elderly man said, "It's gout, young man, quite painful this time."

"They probably got a medicine for that," said Topher.

"I've been to every chemistry shop in Philadelphia, and have yet to find a proper restorative."

Topher heard muffled arguing on the ground floor—something about John Hancock and this place not being the State House.

Topher said, "Sounds like one of youse is an angry drunk."

"Sober, or in his altitudes, John is most often angry. And may I inquire of your name?"

"It's Topher White."

"Your garments are quite curious."

"Same for you. Is that custom?"

"I have a tailor in Philadelphia and a cobbler in Boston, Mr. White. Where were your shoes crafted?"

Topher looked down at his scuffed-up Air Jordans and said, "China, probably."

They reached the middle landing of the tower staircase when lightning filled the tall arched window. A rolling thump of raindrops then quickly trilled into splats against the glass.

Topher heard Juan shout from below, "Keep moving!"

"You can see we're coming!" Topher shouted.

"The Spaniard seems vexed."

"Yeah, that's his default state," said Topher. "Okay, one more flight to go."

When Topher entered Central Hall, he saw Juan herding the four sluggish actors toward the Chestnut Street exit. Two National Park Service rangers—one big, one small opened the door. Behind them was a curtain of rain.

Topher thought, *So much for not getting caught.*

The big park ranger was well over six feet with cropped gray hair and was more muscular than Juan. Topher heard him shout, "We've acquired period-appropriate transport."

Just outside the door, Topher saw a covered carriage. The rapid rain shower pelted its canvas top. Juan handed the other uniformed Park Service ranger the glass container he'd found in Franklin's elevator.

Topher heard the small park ranger say to Juan, "You're late to the party, *hermano*."

Seeing Juan get caught was poetically funny.

Topher shouted, "Ha! Now you're screwed!"

That got their attention.

With a few quick strides, the big park service ranger traversed the vestibule. Topher was afraid he was going to make a tackle, but went to the other side and gently helped with the elderly actor.

Topher asked, "Are you Dave Bautista's father?"

"Show your elders some respect," he said.

"Your master plan just blew up. Great job getting caught," Topher mockingly said to Juan.

Juan didn't seem surprised or scared. He gestured to the small ranger and said, "This is my brother, Jaime."

"Older by five minutes," said Jaime.

Topher said to Juan, "Who's the big guy, your weightlifting partner?"

"That's Michael," said Juan. "No relation. Now stay inside and finish your shift."

"No," Jaime said to Juan. "He can't work with the power out." Then to Topher: "Please help this elderly gentleman into the carriage, *con rapidez.*"

Juan flung his arms wide at Jaime and said, "What would Madame Z say? You think it's best to—"

Jaime asked, "You think it's best to leave him here?"

"I don't think she'd approve of—"

"*¡Coño!* I'm National Park Service *and* your superior tonight."

"That's five bucks for the swear jar," said Juan.

"It's already up to twenty bucks since the power went out," said Jaime.

"I'm cool to stay here," said Topher. "At least it's dry."

Jaime said, "Please, Topher, help him into the first carriage."

Between the wooden door and the horse-drawn transport, Michael held up a large black umbrella with one hand and helped escort two of the actors into the carriage with his other arm.

The actor with the bad knee looked up at Topher and said, "Thank you, young man. You have been very kind."

Topher sensed this geriatric was hurting physically, so he nodded and helped him to the door. Jaimie emerged from the rain, water dripping off his wide-brimmed hat, and said, "Do you need help, Dr. Franklin?"

Topher shot him a puzzled look and Jaime re-turned a nonverbal that said, You're going to play along with this.

"You're getting into the next carriage. And you're still on the clock. *¿Entiendes?*"

"Going where? I'm not done with my shift," said Topher.

"Away from here," said Jaime. "A tavern."

"Looks like they've had enough." Topher pulled his iPhone from his back pocket, but Jaime stopped him. "Don't! Especially around these guys."

"For real?"

"You're working, so put it on vibrate. I got a text from Madame Zaphon—she says they're VIPs."

Topher didn't like how this was going. Janitor pay didn't cover escorting drunk actors to a tavern where they'd get more inebriated. He was mad at Jaime for making him go. He was mad at Madame Zaphon for trapping him in this stupid job.

After helping "Dr. Franklin" into the first carriage, Topher got into the second carriage and sat next to an older white man with black hair. A younger man with red hair sat across from them. How were these guys VIPs? They were just character actors like you saw every day in Central City but smelled homeless. They seemed to get queasier once the horses got moving. If they barf in here, Topher thought, I'm gonna break into Madame Zaphon's office and steal those files she owes me.

The younger actor ran a hand through his red hair and rubbed his eyes. The tall, dark-haired man didn't wear a wig either. Like the Franklin actor, their shoes and clothing were the best he'd ever seen. The buckles on their shoes were metal, not plastic. Most actors around Independence Hall wore cheap costumes and wigs, but these guys looked authentic. Maybe they were from Hollywood. Bored with the silence and bothered by the smell, he said, "I don't think I've seen youse around—you new? What's your name?"

"Roger Sherman," said the man with black hair.

The redhead seemed jolted by the question. "Why, my name is Thomas Jefferson, young Negro."

For the rest of the ride, Topher held back his anger. He thought these actors needed a Red Bull, not more alcohol. They passed City Tavern and stopped at a smaller tourist trap on Spruce Street called A Man Full of Trouble. The wooden placard had the strangest painting: a colonial man and woman walking arm in arm. A man has a parrot on his right index finger and a monkey on the opposite shoulder. A woman hangs a pot on her free arm with a cat on the lid. It was a ridiculous logo that made no sense. What troubled the man? Was his parrot going to referee a fight between the monkey and the cat?

Outside the red-bricked tavern, Jaime got out first, hopped through the rain, and talked to a short, homeless-looking Asian man outside. When Jaime waved them in, Topher let the racist redhead walk ahead and stayed behind with the dark-haired guy named Roger.

Inside, the small room was free of customers. Candles lit every table and wall and decorated a lot like Independence Hall, down to the green table-cloths. The five men fumbled into chairs as the short Asian guy arrived with a tray of drinks in shallow, small-stemmed glasses.

Jaime said to them, "Madeira, gentlemen,"

Thomas drank his in a single gulp while the others stared into their glasses.

Roger pushed the glass away and politely said to Jaime, "I shall take tea, *por favor, Señor.*"

"Of course, Mr. Sherman." Jaime jerked his hand to his pocket and Topher knew it was a buzzing cell phone. Must have been urgent because he turned back to the Asian guy and said, "A tea for the gentleman." Jaime addressed the table and said, "The first round is on me." He then whispered to Topher: "Make sure they drink up. I need to step outside—Madame Zaphon called."

"Sure, whatever, man." Topher didn't like alcohol. The last time he drank was at that underground poker game when his foster brother, Todd, got beat up because the hosts thought they were cheating. After that night and the severe injuries Todd got, Topher swore off drinking.

He felt a buzz in his back pocket. That pulse meant the message was encrypted. "Excuse me, gentlemen. I have to get a message. *Señor* Jaime wants you to drink up."

Topher turned his back to the table, approached the bar, and checked the message. The iPhone was at two percent battery; hopefully, there was enough juice to decrypt the message. It was from a hacker contact he knew on the dark web as Eld0nT, and he wanted to recruit ZooS to finish a complicated identity theft hack. Topher's dark web name was ZooS, a play on the name Konrad Zuse, the German who invented the world's first programmable computer. Eld0nT claimed they couldn't do it without ZooS because only his talents would do. Flattery always helped, but he considered it for half a second before deciding against it. He was finally getting used to breathing with both lungs. Besides, the GED score and new identity were going to get him away from Madame Zaphon and into another legitimate, better-paying job.

Topher was about to send a reply, but stopped when he noticed a disapproving look from the bartender.

He said, "Take this to Mr. Sherman, the dark-haired gentleman." Topher slid the iPhone into his back pocket and picked up the tray. When he arrived, the five colonial actors seemed more sober and conversational.

"Was the message for any of us?" the Franklin actor said.

"No. It was for me. Someone tried to get me in on a job."

The fat, middle-aged actor with rotten teeth said, "What kind of job, young man?"

"Crime, actually." Topher smiled and watched their reactions. Roger coughed into his teacup and the others stared. There was another buzz in his back pocket—a different pulse this time.

"You jest, young man. Hilarious indeed, ha ha!"

Topher mimicked his accent. "No, sir, ye jest not. Or is it jest-me-not?" Then in a normal voice: "They want me in on a scheme to steal identities."

"How do you steal an identity, young man?" Franklin asked.

Roger said, "One's identity should only be in Jesus Christ."

Topher was about to speak when the phone buzzed again. "I'll explain in a moment. Excuse me."

The text must have been from Jaime because it was: MEET ME OUTSIDE. All caps—this National Park Service ranger seems on edge. He looked up and saw the bartender approaching with another tray of drinks. Topher said to the actors, "Look, more alcohol. I'll be right back. Have to check the horses or carriages or whatever outside."

The rain had let up, and Topher found Jaime pacing back and forth like a leopard in a cage.

"What took you so long?"

"First you want me to watch them drink; now you want me outside. Decide, will you?"

"Got a *mensaje*, a message from," Jaime stuttered. "*Ella me preguntó*. She asked me to ask you."

"Take a breath, slow down." Topher raised his arms over his head like a ballerina and took a deep breath, then let it out and lowered his arms. "From the diaphragm. Like this, see?"

Jaime slowed his speech. "Madame Zaphon wants you to take the five actors to Declaration House. Immediately. It's on 7th and Market." Only take carriages. No taxi, no car service. Got it, *ese*?"

"That's a pretty expensive hotel for drunk actors. Why me?"

"Because, Madame Z." Jaime paused and handed Topher an envelope with hundred-dollar bills slipping out. "Look, they're five actors from out of town. And here's your payment. Madame Zaphon said its tax-free cash if you get them there now. Saimon will help."

"Wait, who's Saimon?"

"The bartender."

"He works for Madame Zaphon too?"

"Tonight, he does. So do you. Now get them to Declaration House."

Jaime hopped into a nearby red Ford Boss 302 Mustang and squealed away.

Topher flipped through the envelope and counted off almost two thousand dollars. He smiled. This was a nice parting gift. Once he got those files, Topher thought he'd be done with this job and Madame Zaphon forever.

CHAPTER FOURTEEN

THOMAS JEFFERSON

POOR RICHARD

The scientists from Franklin to Morse were clear thinkers and did not produce erroneous theories. The scientists of today think deeply instead of clearly. One must be sane to think clearly, but one can think deeply and be quite insane.

- Nikola Tesla (July, 1934)

Declaration House - 700 Market St. - Philadelphia, PA - Sunday, June 12th, 2011 - 5:20 a.m.

Thomas Jefferson woke to unfamiliar sounds. He sat up to hear better, but the pain in his head pulsed out of time with the beat of his heart. He thought, *Where am I? How much Madeira did I drink?* Cool air blew through his hair, yet the window next to his bed was closed. A green light filtered through the cream curtains and suddenly changed to yellow, and seconds later, to red. He studied it for several minutes to confirm the pattern.

Green.

Yellow.

Red.

The events of last night were unclear, including how he arrived in this room. He stood to approach the window when John Adams appeared in the doorway.

"Mr. Jefferson, thank God you're here, sir!"

"Ahem, yes, Mr. Adams. What seems to be—"

"How did we arrive in this place? I cannot remember anything except Dr. Franklin's Bell Lift Cage." Adams rubbed his temples. "My head feels as if it shall burst."

Thomas couldn't remember anything from the prior evening. He said, "Why would we have been in the bell tower of the State House?"

"I did not rent a room with you, did I?" Adams asked.

"I took up lodging at Jacob Graff's house."

Roger Sherman and Robert R. Livingston, two other members of the committee, entered the room.

Adams approached them and said, "Do either of you remember the events of last night or how we got here?"

Roger walked to a nearby portrait hanging on the wall, pointed to it, and said to Thomas, "Have they transported us your Virginia estate? This appears to be your father. Quite a likeness."

"It's too dark to see anything," said Adams.

"Mr. Sherman," said Thomas, "Travel to Virginia requires a fortnight, not an overnight." He stared at the portrait and saw it couldn't be his father. The man's hair in the painting was white, not black as tar.

Adams redirected Thomas's attention. "What's the meaning of these colored lights?"

Thomas pulled back the curtain, gasped, and said, "My eyes deceive me. A bright yellow carriage moves without a horse."

The others crowded around to see it. Next to the horseless carriage was a pole with three lanterns attached, each covered with a different colored lens: green, yellow, and red. They were lit and extinguished without the aid of a lamplighter.

"How is this so?" Thomas asked.

Roger said, "Perhaps Dr. Franklin could surmise its inner workings."

"Yes, Dr. Franklin!" said Adams.

Roger disappeared into the hall, returned, then said, "All the bed chambers are vacant; perhaps Ben is on the ground floor."

Thomas and the others moved toward the door except for John Adams, who stared into the middle distance and said, "This must be a dream. The lamps, the carriage, the portrait, this room—"

Thomas suddenly remembered something. "We were at a tavern last night. Dr. Franklin was with us."

"Yes, we had a late-night tea," said Roger. "Sadly, no biscuits."

"What tavern?" Adams demanded.

Thomas said, "It was called A Man Full of Trouble."

"I faintly remember it," said Adams.

"Please, Mr. Adams," said Thomas. "Make haste and accompany us to the lower level. Perhaps Dr. Franklin is here and has a recollection of last evening."

They clomped down the wooden steps and met a young woman wearing an apron in the hallway.

She sounded African. "Good morning, gentlemen. How may I be of help?"

"Have you seen Dr. Franklin, miss?"

"Yes, sir, Mr." She looked with expectant eyes.

"Jefferson, Thomas Jefferson."

"He is down the hall in the Graff Suite."

"This is not Jacob's house," said Thomas.

"We are in Declaration House, gentlemen, which is sometimes called Graff House. I am Makena Karega, your concierge. You may call me Kae."

Thomas translated the French word and said it aloud, "Caretaker."

"Are you taking him to Christ Church after break-fast?"

"It is not Sunday. Yesterday was Tuesday," said Thomas, his head clearing. "Therefore, today must be Wednesday, June 12th."

Kae said, "Yes, sir. Today is June the 12th, but it is Sunday."

The desk lamp pulled Thomas' attention more than the day of the week. He peered under the shade and said, "How can this candle produce a bright light while enclosed in glass? I see no wax or kerosene. What's fuels it?"

Thomas lifted the lamp over his head, and the others twisted their necks to look beneath the shade.

Kae broke the silence when she answered, "Elec-tricity."

Thomas and the other men turned to Kae.

"It uses electricity for fuel," said Kae.

"Dr. Franklin," said Adams. "This must be one of his inventions. Where does he find the time to make these?"

"Let us ask him ourselves," said Thomas.

When they entered the unlit room, Dr. Franklin lay so still Thomas thought he was dead. He shook his shoulder and said, "Dr. Franklin. Dr. Franklin. Benjamin. Ben?"

His eyes parted slowly, and Thomas exhaled in relief.

Dr. Franklin said, "Thomas, Roger, John, Robert. Gentlemen, you look upon me as if I am lying in repose." He ran his hand across the quilt. "If so, it is quite comfortable." He struggled to sit up, so Thomas and Roger helped him upright.

Thomas said, "Accept our apologies for waking you at this hour. They quartered us on the upper floor."

"And what is the matter? The cock has hardly crowed," said Ben.

"The events of last night to me, to us, are unclear," said Thomas.

Simultaneously, the lamps on all four walls illuminated the room, and everyone jumped in shock.

Adams became even more agitated and waved his arms. "You see? The reason none of us remember much from last night is self-evident. We are *still* asleep." Like Hamlet with Yorick's skull, he lifted a pewter mug from the nightstand, held it out, and said, "This is all a hallucination, you see? Everything looks familiar, but many things are strange. From the window, I saw a yellow carriage moving without a horse and a pole of colored lights, lit up as if by magic." He waved his free hand in the air. "And what of this? Frigid wind blows about this room, yet there's no window. Gentlemen, can't you see? None of this is real."

Kae appeared in the doorway with an apple in one hand and a knife in the other.

Adams swung the pewter mug at the bright lamp on the wall, which shattered and sparked. "A room doesn't light itself, and a fire enclosed in glass cannot burn. It breaks with natural law because no such thing exists. Am I wrong, Dr. Franklin?"

Thomas wasn't sure if it was his headache or Adams' diatribe, but nobody in the room responded.

Adams grabbed the knife and apple from Kae, looked at the half-cut fruit, and crunched a bite. "This apple is fresh, yet the harvest isn't until autumn." He dropped the fruit to the floor and continued: "And none of you are real, either. See, I'll prove it!"

Before anyone could stop him, John Adams jabbed the short knife into Dr. Franklin's round belly, jolting wide Ben's gray-blue eyes.

Kae screamed as the room instantly went dark. Thomas didn't know what to think. Maybe this was fantasy. Surely there were members of the British Parliament who wanted to stab Benjamin Franklin, but John Adams had a gift for verbal violence, not physical.

"I'm afraid," Dr. Franklin gasped, "'tis quite a painful hallucination."

The room lit up again. Kae stood in the doorway, her mouth open. Blood dripped from the blade onto the quilt as an ever-expanding red circle oozed from the puncture site.

"Get me to Pennsylvania Hospital," said Dr. Franklin. "Tell Dr. Rush there's no need for bloodletting this time. I shall arrive pre-bled."

"Ms. Kae, call for a carriage, *s'il vous plaît*," said Thomas. "Make haste!"

Kae left, then reappeared at the door and spoke into a makeup container: "700 Market Street. My name is Makena Karega. Please hurry." She closed the makeup container and said, "Help is on the way."

Adams stood in the corner and dropped the knife to the wood floor while Roger removed his shirt and placed it over Dr. Franklin's wound.

This was turning into a nightmare. Thomas felt a strong need to get back to reality, to something familiar that could extract himself from this madness. No longer would he be an unwitting player in this bizarre production, so he resolved to change it here and now. He announced, "Gentlemen, Mr. Adams is so consumed this is not reality that we must have lost sight of our committee's purpose."

Roger said, "What do you propose? Dr. Franklin requires a physician."

Thomas said, "We are the committee responsible for writing a declaration, a document that will define the reasons we must separate from Great Britain. Mr. Adams, you and your cousin Sam know these reasons firsthand."

Adams stared at the floor and did not make eye contact.

"Please, Mr. Adams. John," said Thomas. "I propose you refocus your mind and turn this dream from bad to good, one with a productive outcome."

"How?"

"I recommend you write the declaration."

"I will not. You should do it."

"No? Why will you not do it?"

"Why? There are enough reasons."

"What can be your reasons, Mr. Adams?"

"There are four. Reason first, you are a Virginian, and a Virginian ought to appear at the head of this business. Reason second, I am obnoxious, suspected, and unpopular. You are very much otherwise. Reason third, you can write ten times better than I can."

John Adams broke eye contact and turned his gaze to the bloodied knife on the floor.

Thomas took a step closer and said, "Mr. Adams. You said there were four reasons."

Staring at the floor, he said, "Reason fourth. I may have just mortally wounded Dr. Franklin."

CHAPTER FIFTEEN

TOPHER WHITE

ROUGH DRAFT

That all Men are born equally free and independant, and have certain inherent natural Rights, of which they can not by any Compact, deprive or divest their Posterity; among which are the Enjoyment of Life and Liberty, with the Means of acquiring and possessing Property, and pursueing and obtaining Happiness and Safety.

\- George Mason IV (May 20th, 1776)

Declaration House - 599 S 7th Street - Philadelphia, PA - Monday, June 13th, 2011 - 8:35 a.m.

Smashing the GED was Topher's golden ticket out of his conscripted service to Madame Zaphon. He believed she would accept it in good faith, and she even agreed to meet in person. The paper files she held ransom were the only remaining evidence of his old name and upbringing in Philadelphia Social Services. After this meeting, Topher was ready to start his new life with the new identity he had earned.

Declaration House was a strange choice for the meeting. He had figured the contract with Madame Zaphon would end where it had begun: her office in the Penn Mutual building. He didn't mind the venue choice when Makena Karega, the concierge at the boutique hotel, opened the door. She had dark, flawless skin, full lips, and natural hair. A waft of Shea butter hooked his nose, probably a leave-in conditioner. She was a natural beauty; Topher couldn't tell if she even wore makeup. Even the drab, loose-fitting colonial dress complimented her subtle curves. She was the complete opposite of what his foster brother, Todd, found attractive: girls who straightened their hair, wore way too many cosmetics, and squeezed into uncomfortably revealing clothes.

This woman, much like the past few days, was unexpected.

"It's you again, Mr. White." She had an African accent.

"Please, call me Topher."

"And you may call me Kae."

"I'm here on business to meet Madame Zaphon."

"A Philadelphia treasure," said Kae. "She's expecting you, and you're late."

The compact foyer had only a desk on the left, where Kae resumed her position opposite the three high-backed wooden chairs in the waiting area. Madame Zaphon perched in the middle seat with the alert posture of a peregrine falcon.

Her presence frightened Topher more than the Trueno twins, who stood rather than sit on either side of Madame Zaphon. Juan wore the black and white Quercus Security clothes, and Jaime donned the green National Park Service uniform.

Nobody smiled.

"Why the grim faces?" Topher asked. "Is this a hotel or a funeral parlor?"

"There's been an accident," said Juan. "One actor you brought here is in the hospital."

"Sorry to hear, but they were fine when I left. Drunk, maybe, but not hurt." Topher removed the paper with his GED score from his back pocket and handed it to Madame Zaphon.

"What is this?" she asked.

"Termination of my services to you and this job. Contract fulfilled. I passed the exam and now you can hand over my files, as promised. That's why you called me here, right?"

Madame Zaphon unfolded the paper and examined it slowly before she said, "A perfect score, Mr. White. Well done."

"That means we're done."

"Not exactly," said Jaime, the shorter, much thinner twin. "The Park Service wants the names of everyone in the building before and after the power went out. Those actors breached security, and they're looking for someone to blame."

"I'm just the janitor," Topher said. "Not security."

"But you were in the building," said Madame Zaphon.

Topher pointed at Juan. "Yeah, but muscle-cop here was the one who found them. If anyone here is to blame, it's—"

"—Mr. White," Madame Zaphon interrupted sternly. "I'm willing to keep your name off the Park Service's list, but only if you can help me."

"With what?"

"Security."

"Say again?"

"The five, now four, men checked into this hotel are VIPs and require twenty-four seven protection."

"Juan's already here. He can do it."

"He needs to be with the others at Pennsylvania Hospital. I'm short-staffed and need you at Declaration House to work as private security."

"What if I refuse?"

Jaime said, "Then you'll have to answer a lot of uncomfortable questions from the Park Service."

"You'll stay on the payroll," said Madame Zaphon. "And with a fifteen percent raise in pay. Do you accept?"

"What about the wad of cash Jaime gave me last night?"

"Consider it a bonus for staying on," Madame Zaphon said.

Topher tugged at the end of his compression shirt sleeve. "My choice is to get in trouble with the feds or to take a new job. What about the files?"

"You'll get them after the actors leave."

"When?"

"They must leave before the 2nd of July."

Topher gestured to Juan. "Do I have to dress like the Spanish Schwarzenegger here?"

Juan said, "We're Cuban, *yuma*."

"Don't care," said Topher.

Madame Zaphon said, "The uniform is optional, but you must start today, at this moment."

Topher had enough of this. His first impulse was to walk out the door without saying another word. He'd have to disappear physically and conjure up some other identity. But then he looked back at Kae, who had obviously heard the entire exchange. She gave Topher a look that seemed to say, You're an idiot if you don't take this deal from the crown jewel of Philadelphia. Topher then viewed this situation differently when he noticed a depth of intelligence in Kae's eyes that added to her allure. Perhaps this job offer would yield benefits other than a pay increase and a relaxed dress code.

"Okay," Topher exhaled. "I accept, but after July 2nd I get those files and I quit for good."

"Understood," said Madame Zaphon, who then stood abruptly and left with Juan and Jaime.

When the door closed, Topher noticed Kae's expression had changed to an angry one.

"What's wrong?"

Kae said, "Stage actor or not, Mr. Snodgrass upstairs has taken his role too far."

"Why?"

"There was a chamber pot outside his door, and someone had *used* it."

A youthful voice from the back of the hall said, "That's just nasty. Glad I didn't see it." A tapping white cane announced her approach.

"I could've saved it for you," said Kae.

"Again, nasty. Speaking of, there's a new smell in the room. Who's here?"

"I was talking to Mr. Christopher White, the new guard."

"The name is Topher, not Christopher."

"This is my sister, Fumnaya." Kae gestured to the smiling girl who had darker skin than Kae and long, braided hair that hovered above her shoulders. Her African accent was present, but not strong.

Fumnaya said, "I, ahhh, sorry. I didn't mean to say you smelled. I mean, not like the old guys upstairs. Phew! They need a bath." Fumnaya held out her hand. "Pleased to meet you, Topher."

He stepped forward and shook it awkwardly.

Kae said, "The men checked in must be famous if they require security."

Fumnaya moved uncomfortably close to Topher. He'd never met a blind person before, so he let it pass. The young teenager was a gum chewer and used the same leave-in conditioner as her sister.

"Yeah, and the loud guy stabbed the old guy," said Fumnaya. "Stuck him like a Thanksgiving turkey."

Topher stepped back and said, "Nobody told me about an assault. Did someone break in? They catch the guy?" He tried for a professional tone, but the saggy jeans, long-sleeved compression shirt, and blue hoodie didn't give the look.

"It happened in the Jacob Graff Suite early yesterday morning." Kae Pointed. "Down that hall."

"Did they arrest the guy?"

Kae said, "The conflict was internal, a friendly stabbing. In my view, it was an accident fueled by alcohol and poor judgment, most likely in that order."

"Great," Topher scoffed. "I'm not protecting these VIPs from anyone breaking in. I'm protecting them from themselves."

"Indeed, Mr. White. Now it's been awfully quiet upstairs. Mr. Snodgrass is the only one here."

"Which one's that?"

Kae said, "The one with ginger hair."

That was the last person Topher wanted to see.

Fumnaya grabbed Topher's arm and said, "I'll show you where."

He wasn't sure what to do. A blind girl was leading him up the stairs. Topher believed it should have been the other way around. Before he could react, they were halfway there.

Topher knocked when they got to the door.

No response.

Then he shouted, "Anyone there?"

"Enter," said a squeaky voice.

Inside, the redhead hovered over a wooden lap desk. He held a feather in his hand and still wore the same costume.

"Good morning," said Topher.

For nearly thirty seconds, Topher watched the actor stare at scribbles on a sheet of brownish paper before there was a response: "I am famished. Are you here with my breakfast?"

"Food? No, you don't understand. My name's Topher White, and I'm here for private security."

The teenager squeezed around Topher and said, "Hi, Mr. Snodgrass. I'm Fumnaya. My sister, Kae, is the concierge and can order you breakfast."

"Snodgrass?" The redhead appeared puzzled.

"What would you like to eat?" Fumnaya asked.

"I fancy muffins, hot wheat or corn bread, some cold ham, and butter. Yes, and tea with cream and honey. No, I shall try coffee. Dr. Franklin speaks highly of it."

"Got it. No problem, sir." She unfolded a white cane and left.

Topher used this opportunity to get away. "Need help with the stairs?"

She went on without stopping. "Nope—been up and down these since I was twelve."

Topher took a long, cleansing breath and stared at the racist, feather-toting freak.

He stared back at Topher and said, "Why are they calling me Snodgrass? My surname is Jefferson, Thomas Jefferson."

Topher fought the urge to roll his eyes and said, "Why're you here alone? All your friends are at the hospital."

"I care very little for bloodletting physicians."

"That's probably the only thing we agree on." Topher touched the keloid scar bulging from his chest through the compression shirt. The wound had healed but left a bumpy reminder of his near-escape from Pennsylvania Hospital. He pointed to the paper. "What's that?"

"It's nothing, really—committee work to occupy my mind."

As Thomas dipped the feather into an ink bottle, Topher took a snapshot of the paper in his mind—something he'd always been able to do. He could read it in his head right away, or file it off and bring it back weeks, months, or years later. No delete bin. It was useful for Philadelphia bus and train routes or recalling the countless computer programming books he'd checked into his hard drive of a brain. When he had to prepare for the GED, Topher discovered knowledge beyond assembly languages, kernel programming, and encryption protocols. There was math, science, literature, and even history. Some of it was even interesting.

The curve of Thomas's writing triggered a memory from a book he'd cataloged one sunny afternoon at the Free Library on 7th Street, so he read the snapshot of what the actor had written in his mind, which was:

> *A Declaration of the Representatives of the UNITED STATES OF AMERICA, in General Congress Assembled.*

> *When in the course of human events it becomes necessary for a people to advance from that subordination in which they have hitherto remained, & to assume among the powers of the earth the equal & independant station to which the laws of nature & of nature's god entitle them, a decent respect to the opinions of mankind requires that they should declare the causes which impel them to the change.*

This actor was taking the whole Thomas Jefferson role way too seriously.

Thomas lifted the quill and said, "Did you say you shall serve as my sentry?"

"Yeah. Private security, but without the uniform or stupid hat."

"Indeed, and what is your surname?"

"I told you, it's White, Topher White."

"Well then, Mr. White, this is not the Jacob Graff's house I remember. The furnishings are familiar, yet they're not. Quite a paradox." Thomas pointed at the bathroom. "Is that an indoor privy?"

"Excuse me? A what?"

"A necessary or water closet," said Thomas. "But this one doesn't yield a foul odor."

Topher thought, *You don't smell too great yourself.* But he said, "Yeah. I pissed Kae off about the chamber pot. Use the toilet from now on."

He appeared puzzled and opened his mouth as if to say something, then closed it. Then he set aside the writing materials, stood, and pointed at the light bulb on the wall that was molded to resemble a flickering, burning candle. "And what of these lamps on the walls? None of them have oil, yet they produce light without heat. How is this possible?"

"Ahh, electricity. Dates back to 1746 when Ben Franklin discovered it. That's what powers the lights."

"Yes, Dr. Franklin. How fares he?"

"I don't know, but I'm sure Kae can find out."

Thomas went back to the paper. "I must continue writing."

"Is this some kind of rehearsal for your part?" Topher wondered if Thomas was the one who had stabbed the Ben Franklin actor and felt guilty about it.

Thomas reached into his coat and handed Topher a folded piece of brown paper. "I'm trying to write Section 1 from memory."

Topher opened it and spoke the title: "The Virginia Declaration of Rights."

"My colleague, Mr. George Mason, wrote this. You can read, Mr. White?" Thomas asked in a condescending tone.

Topher thought, *He remembered my name, but still managed an insult.*

"I can write too, mostly code," said Topher.

"Then please indulge me and read Section 1," said Thomas, arms behind his back.

Topher didn't need to look at the paper again to read it aloud, which was:

> *That all men are by nature equally free and independent and have certain inherent rights, of which, when they enter into a state of society, they cannot, by any compact, deprive or divest their posterity; namely, the enjoyment of life and liberty, and pursuing and obtaining happiness and safety.*

He handed the paper back and said, "I'll go check on your breakfast."

Everything about this guy was weird and uncomfortable. He carried around boring old political documents and wrote with ink and a feather. Topher wanted to leave, but he watched Thomas scribble the next sentence on that brown piece of paper, which was:

*We hold these truths to be sacred & undeni-
able; that all men are created equal & independant, that from that equal creation they
derive rights inherent & inalienable.*

Involuntarily, the hairs on Topher's arms poked through his gray compression shirt. He recalled an old book from his GED studies by Julian P. Boyd about the Declaration of Independence and compared it to the next line as Thomas scratched it out:

*among which are the preservation of life, &
liberty, & the pursuit of happiness.*

He realized that not only was this man acting like Thomas Jefferson, but he also wrote with the identical penmanship.

Topher came out of his mind's memory bank and noticed Thomas looking at him strangely.

"Have we met before today?" Thomas asked.

"We met in the carriage, remember?"

"Ah, yes. You're that young Negro boy. Your attire is strange."

Topher tugged a sleeve over his wrist. "Don't call me that," he said with the most control possible.

"Call you what, Negro? My mistake. You're clearly a mulatto. Was your father or mother English?"

Topher raised his voice. "The President of the United States is a mulatto. Which nobody says, ever."

"John was right. This really must be a dream."

"Say what?"

"I meant no offense, young man. We are in Pennsylvania; therefore, you must be a free man."

Anger rose in Topher's chest at the same time he pulled back his fist. He wanted to land it on the bridge of that smug actor's face, but someone grabbed his wrist. It was Saimon, the guy who had helped bring these drunk actors here.

Saimon whispered, "It's not worth it."

"Why?"

"He's not who or what you think he is."

CHAPTER SIXTEEN

GIOVANNI ROSSO

GOLDEN GUINEAS

The truth is, successful investing is a kind of alchemy. -George Soros (From: The Alchemy of Finance: Reading the mind of the Market, 1987)

Giovanni Rosso's Office - 40 Wall Street, 75th Floor - New York, NY - Tuesday, June 14th, 2011 - 8:30 a.m.

G iovanni Rosso studied the largest, most flaw-less blue sapphire he'd ever made under a jeweler's loupe. This one had the potential to impress the world and increase his fame, but he couldn't unveil it until the next month's international gem convention. Rare coins would suffice until then, and Rex Purson was the perfect man for the distraction.

"I got a tip from the Inquirer," said Giovanni.

Rex stared into the Davidoff Géant humidor and grunted, "What Inquirer?"

"The Philadelphia Inquirer."

Rex picked up a cigar and rolled it under his nose. "Don't bother, Herr Rosso. Newspapers die in the mid-twenty-first."

"Why purchase the establishment when you can buy the staff's loyalty? My generous donations have benefited editors, columnists, and photographers across this country."

"So?"

"It allows them to thrive in their craft, and all I ask in return is information. They feed me stories that fit my self-interest well before they're published."

"What's it this time?"

Giovanni swiped at his Galaxy S II to show Rex a photograph. "I told my beneficiary to hold this story."

Rex scoffed. "Coins, Herr Rosso?"

"Thirty George the Third guineas, and in mint condition. They showed up at a Center City gold exchange."

"What's so special about them? You've got vaults filled with bullion."

"Look closely." Giovanni pinch-zoomed the image to magnify it. "These were minted in England between 1770 and 1773 and verified authentic by two Philadelphia experts on 18th century coins."

"You can get these anytime."

"These are unique because they've never been chemically treated."

"What's your point?" Rex clipped the end of a rare Cuban cigar with surgical precision.

"The owners simply traded them for the current market price of gold."

"So?"

"They're worth triple that on the rare coins market," said Giovanni. "The world hasn't seen specimens like these in over a hundred years."

"Get to the point."

"I want them."

"I have a better idea. Let's go back to *Schloß* Louisenlund, use the time cage, and get our own George the Third coins, fresh from the mint."

"Philadelphia is much closer, and the coins are here in 2011."

"You own a private jet."

"Not possible. I was all over Europe in the 1770s and you know the cage would kill me if I went back to that time," said Giovanni.

"Corbin and Phineas can get them," said Rex.

"No. Your particular set of skills is required for this one."

"Why?"

"The sellers didn't leave an address, and you're better than anyone I know at finding people with little to no information."

"I take it you have no leads," said Rex.

"My source also sent me this video feed from the gold store." Giovanni swiped and played a grainy ten-second video. In it was a dark-complexioned African girl and a short, fat, middle-aged man.

"Send that to me," said Rex.

"Find them. And if there are more coins, buy them out."

"What if they don't want to sell?"

"Bring them to me here in New York."

"To what end?"

"Unlike you, I can be persuasive and charming."

CHAPTER SEVENTEEN

TOPHER WHITE / CORDELIA BEGEISTERT

METHOD ACTING

We differ, blind and seeing, one from another, not in our senses, but in the use we make of them, in the imagination and courage with which we seek wisdom beyond the senses. - Helen Keller, From: *The World I Live In* (October, 1908)

Pennsylvania Hospital - 800 Spruce Street - Philadelphia, PA - Tuesday, June 14th, 2011 - 8:30 a.m.

Topher's near assault on that racist Jefferson actor got him reassigned to Pennsylvania Hospital watching the other actors. If it weren't for Saimon's intervention and calm, logical persuasion, the police would have been called. An arrest record attached to his new identity wasn't a good start, Saimon had reasoned.

Topher was glad to be away from Jefferson, but this change of scenery and uncomfortable assignment made him feel trapped. He hated hospitals and dreaded being there until he saw Kae standing outside the hospital room's door. She wore a purple T-shirt and flattering blue jeans, a big upgrade from the baggy, drab uniform she wore at Declaration House. Topher hoped she'd notice the new short curls with a fade he'd gotten, much better than the bushy, uneven hair he had when they first met.

Topher played it cool when he approached. "What brings you here?"

"I wanted to check in on Mr. Saunders. The question is, why are you here?"

"Juan's back at the hotel with your sister and that actor handwriting the Declaration of Independence with a feather. I'm here to pick up the three visitors."

"Officer Trueno is taking your post at Declaration House?"

"He's a rent-a-cop, not an officer."

"At least he *wears* a uniform."

Topher ignored the jab at his blue hoodie and sagging jeans.

"Why'd you allow your sister to stay back there with that intolerant redhead?"

"How I conduct my business is mine, Mr. White. I was there when the incident happened; I'm the one who called 911; and I spent most of the day here when Mr. Saunders was in surgery. Fumnaya had no problems with Mr. Snodgrass on Sunday. I doubt she'll have any issues today."

"I suppose, but he's a—"

"You have barely been present since dropping them in my care, so you haven't yet earned the right to an opinion." She sighed. "The old man is charming. Reminds me of Jabali, my father. God rest his soul."

When Topher grabbed the door handle, Kae placed her hand over his. Their noses almost touched, and he noted her brown eyes were even more beautiful up close. An odd feeling flashed in his chest, almost like the pain from that gunshot wound, only different.

She whispered, "Yesterday, Mr. Saunders insisted on paying for the surgery with gold coins before he'd let another doctor see him. He also made them move his bed next to an open window, insisting fresh air would speed his recovery."

"So, he's crazy like the ginger, right?"

"Eccentric, perhaps. But they were real gold coins, not fake. Mr. Adams and I exchanged them for cash at the gold store on 8th Street."

"You're playin'."

"They tested them. Each was 22 karats."

"What?"

"The store paid out thirteen thousand dollars, cash. I've never held that much money in my life."

Topher's eyes went wide. Something wasn't right about this. He saw plenty of men wearing costumes around Center City, but he doubted any of them carried real gold coins.

"That's what paid for this private room," said Kae.

Topher opened the door and saw the other actors, still in their costumes, consumed in a lively debate around the patient, but they stopped talking when he and Kae entered the room.

The short, pudgy man was the first to speak. "Miss Karega, what *is* this place? The truth, please. We are no longer in Philadelphia." He pointed at the flat-screen television. "There's a portrait on the wall with moving pictures, and fantastical creations surround Doctor Franklin on this most unusual bed. Yesterday, I took in carriages, structures, attire, noises, and smells unfamiliar."

Topher was glad they didn't direct the question at him. This guy was better than any of the lame actors who gave tours outside Independence Hall. He stole a look at Kae and noted a tiny smile, not quite a smirk.

"Mr. Adams, if I may," said the patient, who was sitting up in the hospital bed next to an open window. "I've deduced three possibilities to explain the sounds, surroundings, and." He gestured to Kae and Topher. "New friends. The first possibility is that John is correct. This is all a dream, albeit fanciful and elaborate." He patted his belly. "Painful, I may add. The second is that one of us has died and this is the afterlife. The third is the simplest but most perplexing. Inconceivable as it may sound, let us assume the newspapers and moving portrait that hangs on the wall are telling the truth, which is this: Although today is June the fourteenth, the year isn't 1776."

"I fail to take your meaning, Dr. Franklin," said the pudgy man.

"We've made a jump in time, 235 years to be exact. It was three days ago when, in a flash of lightning, we left 1776 and arrived in the year 2011."

Topher thought, *Maybe they're rehearsing for a time travel movie.*

"May I offer another possibility, Dr. Franklin?" said a tall, middle-aged man with dark hair. "Perhaps this is the work of God, and He is giving us a vision of a future Philadelphia."

That set off a debate between the pudgy man and the patient on predestination versus free will, and they seemed to have forgotten Kae and Topher's presence.

Topher touched Kae's elbow and walked her to the quietest corner of the room. Her dark skin was as soft as it was beautiful. Once there, he whispered, "It was weird back at Declaration House with the guy who says he's Thomas Jefferson, but these guys are just as strange. There's something seriously wrong."

Kae said, "It's called method acting. They stay in character constantly when preparing for a role, even offstage or off camera."

"That's not a thing."

"It is. My friend pretended to be deaf and blind for three weeks preparing to play Helen Keller in The Miracle Worker. She's a theater major at Penn where I attend university. I can't tell you how many questions she had for Naya."

"Who's Naya?"

"My sister, Fumnaya."

"Something doesn't add up. Their costumes look and smell like they're from 1776, and who walks around carrying 13K in gold?"

"I don't know. Perhaps it's a big-budget movie," said Kae.

"I don't go to movies much. So, who're they supposed to be, anyway?"

Kae pointed discreetly. "The old man in the bed has the role of Benjamin Franklin, of course. The loud short one plays John Adams, first Vice President of the United States and second president." She made a knife motion. "The stabber."

"Didn't he shoot the guy on the ten-dollar bill?"

"No. That's Aaron Burr, different vice president. He must not be in this production. The tall one with dark hair who said God is showing them the future is

Roger Sherman. He was a senator from Connecticut who signed all of America's founding documents."

"And the tall guy with the pointy nose?"

"Robert Livingston, New York senator and the first to administer the presidential oath of office to George Washington."

"Franklin, Adams, and Jefferson are easy, top of mind," said Topher. "But I'd have to go in my brain's hard drive to recall Sherman or Livingston."

"Last semester, I did a study on the jurisprudence of the founding generation. My major is political science."

"How about going out for coffee or something so you can tell me more about these guys? Maybe we could go to a movie." That didn't come out as smoothly as it did in his mind.

"You're working, and I have other arrangements."

"Sometime else then." Topher then pulled a sheet of paper from his back pocket and handed it to Kae. "These are the names they used to check in at Declaration House."

"I was there," said Kae

"Strange thing, though. I can't find anything on the identities of these guys, Richard Saunders or Thomas Snodgrass. None of these actors come up on IMDb or the Internet Broadway Database."

She glanced at it and said, "Famous people often use pseudonyms when they check into hotels. The Internet should have told you that."

"Constitution House ain't exactly The Rittenhouse. That's where I'd think rich actors would stay."

Kae sounded defensive. "Declaration House is much more exclusive, always booked years in advance—"

The door suddenly opened, and Saimon leaned in. He waved to Kae, who gruffly shoved the paper back at Topher and exited. In the hallway, Topher saw Kae approach a guy, clearly not a doctor, in a kilt and lab coat.

Topher whispered, "Who's that, Saimon?"

"Kae's boyfriend." Saimon reached for the door handle.

"He got a name?"

"Dr. James Wilson."

"Doesn't look like he works here. What's he a doctor of?"

"Electrical engineering - youngest ever to become associate professor at Penn. Now stay at your post."

As the door slowly closed, Topher spied Kae embracing, then kissing Dr. Wilson, which was received clumsily. Topher felt a pang of jealousy and thought, *How could a white nerd like that attract such a beautiful woman?* He didn't look old enough to be a professor of anything. The guy had long, curly auburn hair and magnetic clip glasses that hung from his neck like an undone bow tie. Most disturbing were the light green plaid kilt and sporran, a leather bag that looked like the fanny packs tourists wore but with tassels. Luckily, he wore long, gray wool socks that covered his calves. Instead of boots or dress shoes, he wore a blue University of Pennsylvania Crocs. A gray T-shirt with the school's shield completed the look. Topher mumbled the motto aloud.

"Pardon me, Mr. White?" said the one playing Roger Sherman. "Was that Latin?"

Topher turned around and said, "Yeah—*Leges Sine Moribus Vanae*. Saw it on a shirt."

The Ben Franklin actor translated: "Laws without morals are useless."

Hours after Topher White entered Benjamin Franklin's hospital room, Cordelia Begeistert waited for him to exit with Adams, Livingston, and Sherman. She looked back to Franklin's surgical notes (which were under the name of Richard Saunders) as they passed by and didn't think Topher would recognize her. She was about to call Madame Zaphon with a report when Topher stopped, turned around, and got her attention.

"You're Dr. Cordelia, right?" Topher asked.

"That's correct, Mr. White," said Cordelia. It disappointed her for being noticed.

"I never thanked you for patching me up."

"How did it heal?"

"Not good—got a big fat keloid." Topher pointed at his chest.

"There are creams and other therapies I could prescribe."

"It's nothing—just another for my collection." He gave her a paper and said, "Madame Zaphon sent me to get them new clothes. Guess their luggage got lost, so she gave me their measurements and a credit card, but I don't know where to get old white guy clothes."

Cordelia put a hand on her hip and said, "Do I look like an old white guy?"

"I didn't mean to say that. It's just—"

Cordelia flipped the paper over and pointed to the address before Topher could finish.

"Didn't see that. Okay—Boyds Philadelphia—1818 Chestnut. I'll get a cab." Topher took back the paper, put it in his back pocket and said, "Thanks."

As he turned away, Cordelia smiled and said, "One more thing, Mr. White."

"Yeah?"

"Don't dress them in anything you'd wear."

"Wouldn't think of it."

Topher turned back to the trio of Adams, Sherman, and Livingston and announced, "We're going clothes shopping, but Mr. Jefferson won't be coming, so you get to pick what he's gonna wear."

Like a trio of arguing goslings, the time-misplaced founders followed Topher.

When they turned the corner and were out of earshot, Cordelia speed-dialed Madame Zaphon.

She picked up after one ring and Cordelia said, "He would've died if this had happened in 1776."

Madame Zaphon asked, "When can he make the trip back?"

"At least two weeks, and the window is closing for me. I need to get back to General Washington in 1776 before the British arrive on Staten Island."

"Perhaps it's best they stay here in 2011. It may not be safe for them in 1776. Jim hasn't found those Brokers with the photon-charged revolvers." Madame Zaphon sounded remarkably calm.

"Who were they?"

Madame Zaphon didn't answer the question, but said, "Retrieve the Leyden jar and have Jaime send you back."

"I'll go tonight."

"Juan and Jaime will protect the founders here in 2011, and Saimon will continue to watch over Topher."

"Isn't it dangerous to keep him close to these people? I mean, what do a bunch of politicians have to do with a computer hacker?"

"Everything, my dear Cordelia. If the Regents are to guarantee America's future, we must preserve its past *and* its present."

CHAPTER EIGHTEEN

TOPHER WHITE

A SUNDIAL IN THE SHADE

*The individual is ephemeral, races and na-
tions come and pass away, but man remains.
Therein lies the profound difference between
the individual and the whole.* - Nikola Tesla (From: Century Illustrated Magazine,
June 1900)

**Pennsylvania Hospital - 800 Spruce
Street - Philadelphia, PA - Wednesday,
June 15th, 2011 - 8:00 a.m.**

During yesterday's clothes shopping trip, Topher should have realized something was
wrong when the bickering among the three actors

stopped. He was too engrossed in the program he was developing on his iPhone, and when he finally looked up, the only trace of the three actors' existence was three piles of pungent costumes and three pairs of buckled shoes. The tailors at Boyds hadn't seen them leave, and they wouldn't let Topher depart until he paid the bill, which was in the thousands. When Topher left the store, his phone buzzed with a text from Saimon—he had found them in Rittenhouse Square park.

He really hoped that misadventure with the VIP actors would get him fired from his post as private security to the old and stinky, as he'd been conscripted into this unwanted job. When he and Saimon arrived at Declaration House, Madame Zaphon stood outside, waiting. She was understandably angry. It was strike two, but instead of giving Topher what he wanted, she made him responsible for the patient.

This will be easy, Topher thought. All I need to do is offend an eccentric old man and I'll be out of this job permanently.

He entered the hospital room abruptly. The patient was awake and reading a Gideon Bible through tiny bifocals next to an open window.

"Greetings, young man. You're not the Spaniard who usually checks in at this hour. What is your name?"

"Topher White, Mr. Saunders."

"Why does everyone call me Saunders? That was a pen name I used ages ago."

Outside the hospital door, Topher convinced himself it'd be easy to tell off an old white guy, but the man's bluish-gray eyes didn't project the same detached malevolence other men of his generation possessed. He had a look Topher couldn't decode, and it threw him off, so he retreated into the doorway and said, "I'll let you rest."

"No, please come in. Sit down. I haven't had a conversation any longer than a minute, and it's always about my heartbeat or body temperature."

Topher realized he could alienate this guy by simply leaving the room and not engaging at all. He grabbed the door handle and made the mistake of looking back.

"Please indulge the request of an old man."

It wasn't a plea, but a kindly spoken invitation that made Topher feel much more visible than he did with the other actors. Perhaps talking to him would reveal some way to tear him down, so Topher pulled the compression sleeves over his wrists and sat in a chair by the door.

"So you're a Bible-thumper, Mr. Saunders?"

"Maybe I look like Poor Richard in this strange bed, but please call me Ben or Benjamin." He then lifted the Bible to the side of the bed and dropped it. The crack of it hitting the tile floor echoed across the room. "Now, that's quite a good thump of the Bible, was it not?"

"Okay, so you're cast as Benjamin Franklin."

"That book is the only thing I'm allowed to read, apparently. I request daily newspapers, but I don't believe the Spaniard understands English very well."

"He's Cuban, not Spanish. Juan understands and speaks perfect English; he's just stubborn."

"Cuban?"

"You know, south of Florida, near the Caribbean."

"Yes, the West Indies. I've always wanted to visit, but the pirate stories have kept me away. Very dangerous indeed."

"Would you like me to turn the TV on?" Topher picked up the remote and pushed the buttons to stop the conversation.

"Turn the teatime on, Mr. Topher?"

"It's just Topher, and I said TV, short for television. That thing that guy playing Adams called a talking portrait when your castmates were here."

"That is a most interesting invention, as are most things in this Philadelphia. But not now. I'd like to speak with another human being. Everyone treats me as if I'm a leper, always rushing in and out."

Topher set down the remote, leaned back in the chair, and sighed. "Okay, but can you stop the method acting thing? I've had enough with the others."

"I've done many things in my life, Topher. But stage acting is not among them."

Topher said, "Okay, I'll play. What do you want to talk about?"

"You. How long have you been a sentry?"

"Less than a week, and it's just for the money. Your producer must have a huge budget."

He pushed the glasses higher on his nose and stared for a long moment. "Is that all you care for, money? Money has never made man happy, nor will it. There's nothing in its nature to produce happiness. I've had no money and I've had plenty, and I believe the more money one has, the more one wants."

"It paid for this private hospital room—did you really pay for it with gold coins?"

"Of course. Sooner or later, the doctor always takes the fee."

Topher scoffed. "I've been poor my whole life and own one set of clothes. You're looking at it. So I won't know if money will bring me happiness until I have it."

"I'm seventy years old and grew up poor in Boston, the son of a soap maker. And among my sixteen siblings, we were raised with little to no money at all. There were days we didn't have a full meal. But when I was your age, maybe even younger, through hard work and determination, I earned a great deal of money."

"Good for you. No, wait—did you say sixteen siblings?"

"I was number fifteen, but that's not the point."

"What is?"

"Having been poor is no shame; being ashamed of it is."

"Never said I was ashamed. Just need money for food and rent. Anything left over goes to hardware and software for my programs. I'm working on some apps that'll make me more money than this security guard job."

"Apps?"

"Short for applications. I'm developing something the world has never seen."

"Are you an inventor?"

"Yeah, you could say that. I write computer programs. Self-taught." Topher held up his iPhone. "I developed an app that extends the battery life on any iOS device."

"I only understand the word 'battery.' And what do you mean by program?"

"Apps are the future—a telephone and computer in the palm of your hand." Topher moved his chair from the door across the room to show Ben the code.

"Is that your chosen trade? Inventor, not sentry?"

"Don't know. Haven't planned that far ahead."

"Hide not your talents, young man; use them. What's the use of a sundial in the shade?"

"Very poetic. Is that one of your lines in the script?"

"It's something Poor Richard said long ago." Ben squinted in pain as he tried to sit up.

"All that stuff is simple for you to say. Most of your life is behind you, and I'm not sure what's ahead of me, that's all." It surprised Topher to be talking about personal things. "I haven't graduated from high school, but I passed an equivalency exam, so I guess that's something."

"Just like you with your mathematical inventions, I taught myself. Never attended college. But money didn't hold me back from learning and constantly improving myself."

"I feel you. On my own, I mastered the use of six languages: BASIC, Java, C, C++, Ruby, and, most recently, Python."

Topher remembered the day he taught himself computer hardware, software, and operating systems when he was a child. The foster "dad" of the month swore at him and said, "If you can fix it, I'll buy you a giant-sized chocolate bar." Topher took the challenge, and getting that early '90s Windows 3.1 personal computer to work became an obsession. He spent hours inside that bedroom closet with only the light of a CRT and computer books found in a dumpster behind Bundy's. When he finally fixed it, there was no candy bar, just another empty promise from a foster parent whose name Topher couldn't even remember. The lazy old man just used it to play solitaire. What a disappointment and a waste of time. But a week later, Topher realized the reward was learning something new, not the promise of candy, so he dragged around an old milk crate to find more broken dumpster computers he could fix. That led to more complex challenges like teaching himself how to write computer programs.

"I said," Ben's voice drew Topher back. "I'm not familiar with any of those languages. I've taught myself Italian, Spanish, Latin, and German. Do you know those?"

Topher laughed out loud and smiled, something he rarely did since working for Madame Zaphon.

"Well, if you're self taught in Spanish, then why don't you understand Juan?"

"He talks too fast; I recognized only three words."

"Must be the painkillers." Topher pointed at the IV bags.

"Yes, and one of those tubes goes up my sugar stick, if you can believe it."

Topher laughed and said, "Yeah, don't even think about pulling it out yourself."

"Enough about me. I'd like to ask you a serious question." He removed his tiny glasses and continued: "All of mankind is divided into three classes—those that are immovable, those that are movable, and those that move. Which are you?"

"I've been on the move as long as I can remember. Gone from home to home. See, I'm one of those orphans that never got adopted. You know, like Oliver Twist."

"I don't know an Oliver Twist. Is he someone you know?"

"No, that's not what I meant. They left me on the steps of this very hospital when I was a baby and never got a permanent home. Foster parents treated me like a paycheck or a punching bag, sometimes both."

"You have no choice in the manner of your birth, nor in those who raise you, Topher. Nobody does.

But that should not define your future. Everyone faces adversity, and it's how you choose to react to it that matters. So when you get into a tight place, and everything goes against you, and it appears you could not hold on a minute longer, never give up. For that is just the place and time that the tide will turn."

"Maybe it will with the cash pouring in from the app I'm writing. Then I'd have enough to quit this job."

"Money itself will not turn the tide, believe me. Because instead of filling a vacuum, money only makes one."

Topher decided not to argue and said, "Great speech, Ben. Is that in the script?"

"I've never written a stage play, much less performed in one. I believe there are three possibilities for my presence here. First, this is all a dream. Second, I've died, and this is the afterlife. And third—"

"You're from 1776. Heard you say that when I was here with Kae."

"What is your conclusion about the three theories?"

"You don't wanna know what I think."

"I'd like an assessment from an inventor."

"Here are the facts I've assembled so far. First, you and four other guys stumble down the stairs of Independence Hall on a stormy night. All youse wear costumes that look like they didn't come off the rack at a Halloween store. Then you check into the most exclusive boutique hotel in Philadelphia without reservations and you carry no luggage or identification, just gold coins to pay for stuff."

"That's a summary. What's your conclusion?"

"More of an observation. You and the others act and talk like you're not from this time. So either you're the five best actors on the planet or." Topher touched the scar bulging behind his compression shirt and stared through the open window. Acid flushed into his throat.

"Or what?"

"Tell me this," said Topher. "Who's on the hundred-dollar bill?"

"No one prints a visage Continental currency."

"Okay, then what face is on the gold coins you used to pay for all this?"

"George the Third's."

Topher was pretty good at spotting facial tics from liars, and Ben didn't show any of the typical tells. A man playing Franklin would definitely boast of being on currency.

"Thank you for indulging an old man, Topher. You are the only one who's been kind enough to converse with me. Perhaps you will come again but smuggle some newspapers and a bottle of red wine. I'd like to know more about the inventions in this Philadelphia."

"I'll be around. You're my new assignment."

He smiled and said, "Fortunate for me."

"Yeah, I got kicked out of Declaration House because I almost hit the guy playing Jefferson."

"Why?"

"He's brought a 1776 attitude, and he thinks any-one who's Black is a slave."

"I don't need a newspaper from this time to know that slavery has long been abolished. But tell me, how is Thomas coming along with the declaration?"

"Saw him writing it."

"Bring me the draft once it's complete. You can help me review it. Then I'll send for Messrs. Jefferson, Adams, Livingston, and Sherman to have the final review. Right now, the only thing in the present that links the five of us to 1776 is that document, and I feel we must complete it if this future Philadelphia is to exist."

Topher left the room without saying goodbye, then stood in the hallway with his head spinning. He massaged the scar on the left side of his chest and tried to absorb what had just happened. An hour ago, his goal was to get out of this job by upsetting the last of these five strange men, but now the reality was less clear. He got out his iPhone, opened Safari, and looked up coins from the 1700s. After he verified that the image of King George the Third was stamped on gold coins from that time, the device fell from his hand, cracking the screen on impact.

Saimon approached and picked up the broken phone.

"I can't believe it," said Topher.

"I remember the night you were wounded."

"Say what?"

"If I hadn't been there, you'd be dead."

"How do I know you were there? Wait. You're the guy who Bruce Lee'd those guys?"

"Sure did."

"You took down the guys who shot me?"

"Hurt them bad, but had to let them go."

"Why?"

"Few survive a gunshot wound to the chest, and stopping the bleeding was much more important."

"That's a lot of data to process, Saimon. Thank you for saving my life, but the thing that's really got me rattled is I think the man in that room really is Benjamin Franklin."

Saimon smirked. "With an IQ of 225, I figured you would've worked that out a lot sooner."

CHAPTER NINETEEN

GIOVANNI ROSSO

FOR THE WANT OF A NAIL

For the want of a nail the shoe was lost, For the want of a shoe the horse was lost, For the want of a horse the rider was lost, For the want of a rider the battle was lost, For the want of a battle the kingdom was lost, And all for the want of a horseshoe-nail. - Benjamin Franklin (From: *Poor Richards Almanack* - June 1758)

Giovanni Rosso's Penthouse - 40 Wall Street, 75th Floor - New York, NY - Friday, June 17th, 2011 - 7:00 a.m.

Giovanni Rosso ignored the slight after Rex tossed a heavy rectangular coin box onto the 1738 Guarneri del Gesù violin. It screeched across the strings like a startled feline and landed on the lower bout of the rare instrument cradled in its carbon fiber case. He opened it, counted the sleeves and said, "There's only thirty. I compelled you to find the owner and get more."

"*Nein*, Herr Rosso. Couldn't find him."

"There must have been fingerprints."

"Yes, but they didn't match any database, domestic or international."

"What about the security footage from the Philadelphia Gold Exchange?"

"Showed a Negro girl and a fat old man. Ran a facial recognition and the only positive ID was Makena Karega, political science undergraduate at the University of Pennsylvania. Got nothing on the other guy."

Rex's laziness waned Giovanni's patience. Students didn't collect rare coins, so it had to be the unidentified man. He stared at the shiny, 22 karat George the Third guinea inside the square, white frame and tried to sound casual.

"They stopped making these in 1786. Beautiful, isn't it?"

"Sure," said Rex.

"I know the heart of the numismatist, and there must be more coins."

"Why's it so important to find this coin collector, Herr Rosso?"

"Nobody will upstage me when this story comes out. You should have found him, got whatever coins he had left, and paid generously for his silence. This acquisition will make me more famous, raise the profile of —"

"Worldly fame is but a breath of wind that blows now this way, and now that, and changes name as it changes direction."

"When have you ever read Dante Alighieri?"

Rex removed the Motorola Droid from his coat pocket and said, "*Ja?*"

Giovanni raised his arms in frustration. "Who could be more important than *me* right now?"

Rex raised a finger, poured a tumbler of Johnnie Walker Blue to the rim, and listened for a dreadfully boring minute before he shouted, "*Scheiße!*"

Giovanni raised his eyebrows. "Excuse me?"

Rex drank half the glass of whiskey, then said, "I don't believe those coins came from a collector."

"Then where?"

Rex clicked over to speakerphone and raised his voice to say, "Astra and Marquis, tell Herr Rosso where you are right now."

"*Je suis sincèrement désolée*, Mr. Rosso," Marquis said in a thick French accent. "We failed at killing Adams, Franklin, Jefferson, and the others. They had protection, someone with twentieth-century weapons. We narrowly escaped and—"

Rex interrupted: "That's not what I asked, *dummkopf!* At this moment, tell us *where* you are standing."

"Philadelphia, near Independence Hall," said Marquis.

"How is this important?" Giovanni asked.

"Because," said Rex, "It would have taken a month and a half, maybe two, to cross the Atlantic in 1776, then another two weeks to arrive by land in Schleswig-Holstein."

It irritated Giovanni that the conversation wasn't about himself. "I don't understand, nor do I care, unless it has something to do with these coins."

Rex said, "Marquis and Astra have returned to 2011, but didn't use the time cage in your alchemy lab."

That roused Giovanni's curiosity.

Rex shouted into the phone, "Explain how you got here?"

Marquis said, "Six days ago, in 1776, we stormed Independence Hall to take out the five targets who just entered, but Andrew McNair tried to stop us. He's the caretaker at Independence Hall and lives there, except he called it the State House and then—"

Rex stopped him. "Get to the how, not the who."

Astra's alto voice took over the call with her bewitching Greek accent. "Let me explain. Marquis skipped the part where a tiny woman dressed as a man broke his trigger finger and kicked his family jewels."

"She shot *you*," said Marquis.

"I came prepared." said Astra. "Wore a bulletproof vest and used a flashbang so I could pull Marquis away from the assault by his flopping turtleneck!"

"Is this going anywhere?" Giovanni demanded.

Rex said, "Patience, Herr Rosso. For once in your life, listen more than you talk."

Astra said, "We couldn't track any of the five targets in the next three days after that lucky girl stopped us. Visited every Tavern. Cased the State House. They were as ghosts. But then we met McNair at the Tun Tavern and our fortunes turned. Luckily, he didn't remember Marquis shooting him. Thought he was struck by lightning that night. And he was more focused on my cleavage and the shots of rum. After paying his bar tab, he offered to show us his quarters in the bell tower, which is when it got interesting. We spotted a cage with a wire connected to a metal rod in the wall, just like ours under Castle Louisenlund. McNair told us Ben Franklin built an elevator during the construction of the State House, but by 1776 it wasn't used anymore."

Giovanni moved closer to the phone so he could hear every word and how they delivered it.

Astra continued: "McNair told us that six months ago, just before Christmas, some skinny old Negro woman delivered a crate with two Leyden jars and a schematic of Ben Franklin's elevator in the bell tower—"

Marquis interrupted, "We asked to see it, so Mc-Nair took us next door to Carpenters' Hall where he showed us a Leyden jar that looks *exactly* like ours, even had four scrolling numbers on top —"

"—So we took it," said Astra.

"You're not suggesting that The Committee of Five used Franklin's..." Giovanni couldn't finish the thought aloud.

Rex filled the silence. "Tell us what happened next."

Astra said, "McNair was so drunk, he passed out. So we left him at Carpenter's Hall and went back to the bell tower and worked until dawn doing experiments. Tried several round-trip tests to 2011 with *our* Leyden jar in Franklin's elevator, but it failed—wouldn't even disappear. We then used the Leyden jar from the crate and it made a round trip. The mouse inside the jar didn't die, so Marquis and I took a chance and traveled from 1776 to 2011."

Marquis took over the story. "When we appeared, two shocked construction workers were in the bell tower. That problem became an opportunity because we needed their clothes to get past the uniformed officers."

"They witnessed your appearance in Franklin's time portal?" said Rex.

"No worries," said Astra. "The power was out when and we covered our tracks. Disposed of their bodies the way you showed us in Lithuania."

"Well done, Astra and Marquis," said Rex. "Bring the Germany Leyden jar and the one you stole from

Carpenter's Hall to Herr Rosso's lab. I must analyze it." He clicked off the call and downed the remaining whiskey.

The only word Giovanni could summon in response to this revelation was: "*Che cazzo.*"

"Giovanni Rosso, the money trader with a mouth of gold, finally utters a curse. Italian, but it's a start."

"You told me our Leyden jar was unique, a prototype you brought from your time in 2052."

"The inventor must have made more after I fled Philadelphia with the one I pilfered."

"Do you really believe five politicians traveled in time from the eighteenth to the twenty-first century?"

"*Ja*. And remember, one of those politicians *is* Benjamin Franklin."

After a long silence, Giovanni said, "Over six months ago, I told you assassinating the founders before they could write the Declaration of Independence was a shortcut. America still exists, and now they're here in our time."

"Clearly, my plan failed, Herr Rosso."

"It's a colossal *puttanata*!" Giovanni sank into the leather chair and loosened his bow tie. "Everything was simpler back in the eighteenth century when we converted lead into gold and chemicals into rubies for fame and profit."

"More like infamy. And you'd complain incessantly without air conditioning."

"Back then, we didn't have time travel and didn't need twelve Brokers to wreak havoc."

"You've conveniently forgotten there wasn't a large city across Europe in the eighteenth that didn't have a warrant out for your arrest."

"True, and I've had a spotless record since we arrived in the twentieth. Not even a parking ticket."

"I've told you, everything gets worse in the mid-twenty-first." Rex removed a Cuban cigar from the humidor and pointed it at Giovanni. "And the political skills you showed with Louis the Fifteenth, Catherine the Great, and Prince Karl of Hesse-Kassel is why I chose *you* to help me bring down America."

Rex turned the leather-wrapped handle of his ebony walking stick, and with a click, removed a wakizashi sword with a high-pitched ring. He held the end of the cigar at arm's length and, with a gentle swipe, removed the tip like a samurai mohel.

"Perfect, every time." Rex sheathed the weapon and locked it shut.

"That's about as impressive as the last 1,369 times you've done that."

"Today it's 1,370." Rex charred the end of the cigar and said, "This belonged to Oda Nobunaga, his personal wakizashi, you know. Stole it from the Tokyo National Museum—"

"—I don't understand your obsession with feudal Japan."

Rex struck a second match, puffed at the cigar, and slowly rolled the smoke from his mouth. "Sulking doesn't suit you, Herr Rosso. Why the sudden touch of sadness?"

"I'm not depressed just perplexed. How did Franklin build a time portal?"

"Franklin may have used Leyden jars for his eighteenth-century electricity experiments, but the two we now have from 2052 contain terrestrial current technology he never could have imagined. Paired with the formulas from the Nikola Tesla's notebooks, it made time travel possible for us."

"I don't care about scientists, only our next move," said Giovanni. "Those coins were obviously from one of the five, so they're here now. We should employ every available Broker to track them down, take away their Leyden jar, and strand them. When that happens, this country will cease to exist. Job done."

"I wish it were that simple."

"Why?"

"Six days ago, when they arrived in the twenty-first, something big should have happened, much bigger than a Chicago butterfly triggering a Tokyo tornado."

"Speak plainly."

"We are the first to travel in time, and since we arrived in 1992 from 1784, I was afraid our presence would have changed the world like the flapping of a butterfly's wings on one side of the world could cause catastrophic weather on the other."

"You never told me this before. Besides, our arrival and my ascent to the financial elite didn't cause global calamity."

"Exactly, Herr Rosso. That's why I recruited the Brokers last year to manipulate events more aggressively, then measure the cataclysm each left."

"Kennedy never got reelected. You changed that."

"A beautiful debut, and the break-in I orchestrated made sure Nixon never finished his second term."

"You failed at killing Reagan—never trust a nutcase."

"*Ja*, the Brokers changed the history I remembered, but whatever we did, it was like throwing a boulder into a stream: the water only flowed around it."

"Less poetry, Rex."

"Disrupting events in the late twentieth didn't bring down this country, and my latest attempt may have caused its founders to arrive in the twenty-first."

Giovanni's eyes went to the whiskey bottles, and he considered breaking his long-standing sobriety. "What do you propose?"

Rex poured a second drink and said, "We wait. Be patient."

Giovanni read the Johnnie Walker bottle and felt disappointed it was a blended whiskey. He then remembered the Macallan 64-Year-Old Scotch whiskey he won at a charity auction for nearly half-million dollars. If he was going to have his first drink in over a decade and a half, it had better be a good one. He opened the etched crystal decanter and poured two fingers neat.

"If I knew you were going to open that," said Rex, "I wouldn't have opened this piss whiskey."

Giovanni took a sip and sighed with pleasure. "This surely is the piss from angels."

"I'll be the judge of that." Rex grabbed a clean glass and poured four fingers.

"And what should I do while we wait for your butterflies?"

Rex said, "Nothing. We study their Leyden jar, *verstehe mich?*"

"Understood," said Giovanni. "Then what, kill them?"

"*Nein.* I've learned my lesson. Assassination could cause an avalanche this time. I'll send Brokers Finn and Corbin to Philadelphia. Once there, they will find them and observe."

Giovanni finished his drink and said, "I believe Ben Franklin has played a bigger role in the invention of time travel than you let on. Bring him to me unharmed. I must be the first to interrogate him."

CHAPTER TWENTY

TOPHER WHITE

SELF-EVIDENT TRUTHS

We hold these truths to be sacred & undeniable; that all men are created equal & independant, that from that equal creation they derive right inherent & inalienable, among which are the preservation of life, & liberty, & the pursuit of happiness...

- Thomas Jefferson (From the Rough Draft of The Declaration of Independence)

Pennsylvania Hospital - 800 Spruce Street - Philadelphia, PA - Tuesday, June 21st, 2011 - 8:00 a.m.

As he balanced the newspapers atop four Starbucks cups, Topher wondered how the founders got anything done if all they did was drink all day. Red wine, a daily staple for Ben, filled two of the four cups; the other two were espresso. Saimon greeted Topher at the hospital room door and let him in.

Inside, Ben Franklin faced an open window with his arms wide open, as if expecting a hug from an old friend.

Except he was alone.

And naked.

Topher looked at Ben's saggy, white butt, then turned back to Saimon and said, "He calls it an air bath. Claims it'll speed recovery."

Saimon held up a large envelope. "Better put the coffee down before you give him this."

"What's that?"

"Jefferson's handwritten draft of the Declaration of Independence and a note to Franklin."

Topher set the cup holder on the over-bed tray and handled the envelope like it was a newly soldered circuit board.

Saimon then gave Topher a wooden stylus with a pointed metal tip.

"What's this?"

"Fountain pen."

"I thought they used feathers."

"The nib on this one is the same size Franklin used in 1776, and don't let him handle the document until after he is both dressed and has had his morning alcohol."

After Saimon left, Topher reminded Ben that Philadelphia didn't need to see that much of Ben Franklin and gave him a robe before they started their morning the same way they had the past several days. Topher would describe and re-explain how computer hardware and software worked, and then Ben would retell stories of his days when he did experiments and came up with his inventions. After the second cup of wine, Ben would settle into reading every newspaper while Topher would finish his triple espresso and scroll through the programming blogs on his iPhone.

There wasn't anything interesting or new online, so Topher shortened Ben's reading time with the question he really wanted to ask: "You haven't told me about your most significant invention, the time machine. And why you used it to visit 2011."

Ben lowered the paper and said, "I have only the most rudimentary knowledge of your ear-phone, and I can only assume that traveling through time would require a significantly more advanced invention than that thing in your hand."

"It's an iPhone, not an ear-phone."

"Because you hold it in front of your eyes?"

"No. The 'i' means the Internet, the worldwide information network I told you about. So, if you didn't invent it, maybe Madame Zaphon did. But why'd she have it bring you guys here? Maybe 2011 is significant. Something is going to happen, and only you and the others can fix it. You know, people in this time always ask, what would the Founding Fathers say if they could see what's happening in our country now?"

Ben stared into his wine-stained coffee cup with a look of disappointment and scoffed. "I'm flattered Americans will remember us in 2011, but calling us Founding Fathers sounds ridiculous, presumptuous even."

"You're avoiding the question, Ben. Every day I bring you stacks of newspapers and you read every word, but you don't ask me questions or offer opinions on what's happening."

"I'm pleased the political cartoon has survived." Ben laughed and said, "The artists draw such big ears on your president."

"Another dodge like that, and I'll put coffee in your cup tomorrow."

Ben removed his tiny spectacles and leveled a penetrating stare before he spoke. "I don't belong here, Topher. And neither do my opinions. On the other side of the world, the Muslims are engaged in revolution. They call it the 'Arab Spring,' but here, in this America, you're at peace. At least that is what I read in your newspapers."

"What do you mean by that?"

"War is when the government tells you who the bad guy is, but revolution is when you decide that for yourself. They took us away at the very moment many of us, especially Mr. Adams, decided it was time for revolution. But if we are to separate from Great Britain, we must get back to my time, to the Second Continental Congress. It's only in my generation where my views on events in the newspapers truly matter."

Topher handed Ben the envelope. "Speaking of, Thomas sent you a draft of the Declaration of Independence."

Ben opened it and read Jefferson's letter aloud:

The enclosed paper has been read and with some small alterations approved of by the committee. Will Doctor Franklin be so good as to peruse it and suggest such alterations as his more enlarged view of the subject will dictate?

"Talk about presumptuous. He writes like he talks."

Ben put on his glasses. "I will require a desk, inkwell, and quill."

Topher rolled the bedside table over, lowered it, and gave Ben the fountain pen.

"And the ink?"

To test it, Topher scratched his new signature on the envelope and thought it strange that Franklin was no longer his middle name.

"It's already filled with ink—just push down and write."

Ben immediately went to editing. Topher didn't interrupt and somehow he didn't to go back to his phone. After several minutes, Ben made loud, dark slashes across a phrase, set down the pen, and said, "We hold these truths to be sacred and undeniable? This isn't a catechism. Truths are based on analytical facts, not faith. Don't you agree, Topher?"

"Never been religious myself."

"That's because science is based on undeniable, self-evident truths that can be proven and observed."

"Agreed. I always live by what I can see."

Ben scribbled above the stricken phrase and read, "We hold these truths to be self-evident." He then went back to the parchment.

The door opened, and Saimon entered the room with a stack of files.

Topher approached him and whispered, "What's that?"

"Preparation for when he checks out."

"When? He can barely walk."

"We only have a week to get ready. Franklin can get physical therapy outside the hospital."

"Why not get him healthy, then send him back to the exact same time he left 1776?"

"That's not how the time portal works."

"Enlighten me and tell me who exactly invented it if Ben didn't. Was it Madame Zaphon?"

"That's need-to-know, but Ben Franklin invented the apparatus that makes it possible."

"The elevator cage in the bell tower?"

"Yes, and it isn't a DeLorean where you punch in an exact date and time of where you're going, only the year."

"Okay. That means if we send them back today, they'll arrive on June 21st, 1776."

"Affirmative. And that document he's editing needs to get back to the Second Continental Congress by the twenty-eighth."

"What if they don't return by then?"

"Not an option. They'd be stuck in the future a full year."

The door popped open, and a well-dressed woman in a business suit entered. She held an iPad to Saimon's face and said with an accent Topher couldn't identify, "I've gotten unexplainable hits on FRA scans across several traffic cams. These results are from five minutes ago, and it's 100% positive IDs on both."

Saimon furrowed his brow and said something angry in Thai, then he said in English: "What's the location?"

"Two blocks away."

"Who's this?" Topher asked.

"That's Matija Bogadan. She created your new identity."

"Great work. Thanks," said Topher.

Matija said, "We need to leave with Franklin *now*. Get him in that wheelchair."

Topher hesitated.

"Just do it," said Saimon. "Never argue with a Croatian."

——✦——

Ben Franklin didn't stop editing the draft Declaration of Independence as Topher pushed him down the hall and into the same service elevator he'd used last year to escape Pennsylvania Hospital. Matija and Saimon entered, but didn't speak until the gate closed.

As they descended, Matija said to Saimon, "Those two ID'd on four separate traffic cams are supposed to be dead."

"I fought them off six months ago. Had a hunch then, but no time for an FRA. Topher was bleeding out," said Saimon.

"The night you found him?" asked Matija. "Why didn't you tell me it was Corbin Raum and Phineas Ophis?"

"No positive FRA means no positive ID," said Saimon. "They looked younger that night, and didn't pop up on any of your regular scans until today."

Topher asked, "What's FRA? You think they're after me?"

"Facial Recognition Algorithm," said Matija. "A program I developed that uses biometrics to map facial features from a photograph or video, then rapidly compares it to our distributed, encrypted databases to find a match."

"That code sounds sick. I'd love to see it," said Topher.

"I doubt they're after you, Topher," said Saimon.

"I believe they're here for Dr. Franklin," said Matija

"That's pretty far-fetched, even for you," said Saimon. "How would they even know Franklin is here?"

"Here's why." Matija swiped on the iPad screen until it displayed a screen capture of a New York TV morning show interview with Giovanni Rosso.

"It's the Jon Hamm of Wall Street," said Saimon. "How's that relevant?"

"Two problems," said Matija. "First, he's talking about a new collection of eighteenth-century gold coins."

"Rich guys like that treat publicity like currency, and the more you have, the more you want," said Saimon.

"Got that right," said Topher. "For old white guys like that, money and fame equals power over other people."

Matija said, "It's relevant because he said he got them from an undisclosed location in Philadelphia, but I'm pretty sure they're the same ones our patient here used at the gold exchange to pay the hospital bill."

Ben scribbled and spoke in the paper on his lap. "Reduce them to arbitrary power? Mr. Jefferson has it wrong because Great Britain has been deliberate, not arbitrary in its attempts to control the American colonies. It's absolute despotism."

Topher asked, "You mean like communism?"

"I'm not familiar with that word," said Ben. "But in my time, King George has power and authority over a global empire, which can be much more dangerous than a man with great wealth and fame."

"I don't know," said Topher. "Wall Street people like Carl Chain and Giovanni Rosso dominate everything today, keeping the poor in their place while their wealth increases."

Saimon said to Matija, "Maybe Rosso getting Franklin's coins is a coincidence."

"That's what I thought initially, but it's also the second problem," Matija pointed at the iPad and said to Saimon. "An offstage altercation interrupted Grant Heatherton's interview of Giovanni Rosso. Look. This guy offstage tried to light up a cigarette and nearly knocked over the intern who tried to stop him. Security approached, but Rosso waved them away, so I figure they're together. After going through all of Rosso's known business associates, I came up with nothing, so I ran the FRA on the offstage smoker and got a hit on someone from the 1860s."

Saimon unleashed a slew of angry phrases in Thai that persisted until the elevator jolted to the ground floor. Before the door screeched open, he said in English, "He was the Count's right-hand man throughout the Succession Prerogative. You *positive* it's him?"

Matija said, "This is the one time I wish my software was wrong."

Matija put her hand on Saimon's shoulder and said, "Follow the logic here. Corbin and Phineas were two of the twelve Brokers under the Count's command while he manipulated the Union and Confederate sides. Back then, the offstage guy was the Broker who was assigned—"

"To invade and deluge us in blood?" Ben said to the parchment in his lap.

Topher rolled Ben out of the elevator and focused on Saimon and Matija's conversation as they followed him.

Saimon said, "We never got a video or photograph of the Count during the Civil War. Not even a portrait. We thought he was made up like Krahang, some boogeyman invented to instill fear throughout the war. And he was very effective."

"I did some cursory research," said Matija, "and there's no public record of Giovanni Rosso prior to 1992. He did an interview after his first big currency trade, and when asked about his past, Rosso claimed that the Siege of Sarajevo took not only his parents, but everything required to establish an identity—photographs, birth certificates, legal documents—everything."

"The media called him the Sarajevo Survivor," said Saimon. "Are you suggesting Giovanni Rosso has been around for almost twenty years but is actually a time traveler and leader of the Brokers, the same person who orchestrated the assassination of Lincoln, and is the one who now is trying to—"

"Invade and destroy us," Ben said as he scratched in the correction. "Sounds less dramatic."

"It's my working theory that Giovanni Rosso *is* that boogeyman," said Matija.

As they exited the hospital and approached Ben's transport to Declaration House, a bright orange Lotus Elise across the street caught Topher's attention. He had never driven a car, but thought that if he ever became wealthy, he'd buy one like that. The fantasy ended quickly when the driver lowered his binoculars. Topher recognized the face and stopped pushing the wheelchair. Behind him, Saimon and Matija were in deep conversation and bumped into Topher.

"Come on, Topher. We need to keep moving," said Saimon.

"The software is solid," said Topher. "Because there's the guys from the alley—the ones who shot me and you Kung Fu'd."

Matija took a picture of the car with the iPad and said, "*Jebote*!"

Saimon said to Matija, "Call Juan and Jaime. We need a different way out of here and better security." Then to Topher: "Take Franklin back into the hospital."

"Come on, Saimon," said Topher. "You could take 'em easy if there's trouble. I'd love to see a rematch."

"No, you wouldn't," said Saimon.

"There, I've finished my edits," said Ben.

"Why not?" Topher asked.

"Because they're much more dangerous than you think," said Saimon.

Matija added, "And they're also time travelers who died in the 1860s."

Chapter Twenty-One

TOPHER WHITE

Cruel War Against Human Nature

Future ages will scarcely believe that the hardiness of one man adventured, within the short compass of twelve years only, to lay a foundation so broad & so undisguised for tyranny over a people fostered & fixed in principles of freedom.

- Thomas Jefferson (June 24th, 1776)

Penn Mutual Building - 510 Walnut Street - Philadelphia, PA - Friday, June 24th, 2011 - 1:00 p.m.

In the three days since evading the guys from the alley outside Pennsylvania Hospital, Topher White helped the Founders move from Declaration House, the boutique hotel, to Madame Zaphon's floor of the Penn Mutual building. He thought it was an overreaction to Matija identifying the men in the orange Lotus Elise and their connection to celebrity financier, Giovanni Rosso.

It was a total quarantine. Topher worked tirelessly to upgrade their computer network and integrate customizations into a custom closed-circuit security system. The offices became eighteenth century bedrooms, and the boardroom transformed into physical therapy space for Ben.

With eyelids feeling like the loose hinges of a laptop, Topher left the security program he was developing and get an espresso from the kitchen. He turned the corner and collided with Kae and her sister, Fumnaya.

"Sorry, didn't see you coming," said Topher.

"That's *my* line," said Fumnaya.

"Blind girl humor," said Kae. "Please excuse her. She wanted to come along and get you."

"For what?"

"You missed lunch, and Mr. Saunders has requested your presence," said Kae. "They're starting rehearsal."

The sisters didn't know the truth about them being the actual founding fathers who traveled from 1776 to 2011. Topher had sworn to keep that secret. Madame Zaphon brought them over from Declaration House to give the guests continuity of care, and Topher was happy to get more time with Kae.

Fumnaya shoved her white cane into Kae's chest and grabbed Topher's arm. "Great! You can escort me."

The cafeteria area became an inviting dining room replete with colonial-style furniture. Because of the bottles of Port and Madeira wine, as well as a nearly depleted bowl of rum punch, everyone seemed in high spirits. An elaborate lunch had been served and plated on fancily patterned dinnerware, not paper plates. Even the utensils were genuine silver, not plastic.

"Go ahead," Kae said to Topher. "I ordered plenty of food."

Topher wrinkled his nose and squinted. "Smells awful."

Kae pointed at each course and described it. "They started with turtle soup and butterhead lettuce with Russian dressing. The main courses are eel pie, roast quail, and smoked ham."

"The only thing I recognize is ham. Why couldn't you order in Tony Luke's and give them a real taste of Philly?"

"Only if you wanted to make them sick."

"And what's that supposed to be?" Topher pointed at the dessert tray.

"You eat Philly cheesesteak but not cheesecake?"

"No, thanks," said Topher as he grabbed a slice of ham and wheat bread. "That doesn't look like cake, and why make one with cheese?"

At the other end of the table, Thomas raised his glass and said, "Ms. Makena and Ms. Fumnaya, you both have been very gracious and kind to me this past fortnight. It's opened my mind and soul to the possibilities of a glorious future where every American, regardless of his, or her, upbringing." He took a sip of Madeira before continuing. "I believe I am trying to say what most of this committee feels."

"Excuse me, Thomas," said John Adams, "but you're not being clear at all. What *are* we feeling?"

Ben belched and said, "I, for one, am feeling quite full. This feast has been exquisite, Kae. Much better than the hospital food."

"Perhaps feeling is not what I intended," Thomas continued. "Believing may be a better descriptor. Stated plainly, this document I've labored over is the only connection I have to the old routines, and perhaps the reason for our experience here is to show us what this declaration will produce, an independent America with free Negroes, one whom later becomes the president of the—"

"African Americans," Topher cut him off. "How many times have I told you that?"

Kae spoke up. "Excuse me, Mr. White. I was born in Kenya, and when my father, Jabali, sought political asylum, he brought me and my sister to the United States and we eventually became legal American citizens; therefore, Fumnaya and I are the only ones in this room who are both African and American."

Kae's correction irritated Topher. "What's wrong with African American?"

"Quite, yes, Mr. White," said Thomas. "These free Africans are a vision of the future this document will fulfill, and that is why I've included this next section as the last reason for our separation from Great Britain." He held up the parchment and cleared his throat before reading,

He has waged cruel war against human nature itself, violating it's most sacred rights of life & liberty in the persons of a distant people who never offended him, captivating & carrying them to slavery in another hemisphere, or to incur miserable death in their transportations tither. This piratical warfare, the opprobrium of infidel powers, is the warfare of the CHRISTIAN king of Great Britain. Determined to keep a market where MEN should be bought & sold, he has prostituted his negative for suppressing every legislative attempt to prohibit or to restrain this execrable commerce and that this assemblage of horrors might want no fact of distinguished die, he is now exciting those very people to rise in arms against us, and to purchase that liberty of which he has deprived them, by murdering the people upon whom he also obtruded them; thus paying off

former crimes which he urges them to commit
against the lives of another.

Topher whispered to Kae, "That's not in the Declaration of Independence, is it?"

"Not to my knowledge."

"I thought you studied political science."

"True, but it is not the same as history."

When he looked up, Topher realized Thomas had stopped reading, and the others stared as if expecting a reaction.

John Adams relieved the silence. "Mr. Jefferson, if I may. This document not only separates the colonies from Great Britain, but do you mean to say it shall abolish slavery from the American colonies upon its very founding?"

Thomas opened his mouth, then shut it again.

Adams continued: "Your boldness makes you worthy of being called a Son of Liberty! Now, tell me this—will your Virginia colleagues and the other southern colonies support this? Will you, Mr. Jefferson, as an example for all, free the slaves you yourself own in this new, independent America?"

"You see the evidence." Thomas meekly gestured to Kae, Topher, and Fumnaya. "They are free, and this break from Great Britain will end the slave trade. Am I right?"

With a quiet confidence Topher rarely heard in others, Kae said, "Yes, the Declaration says that *'all men are created equal, that they are endowed by their Creator with certain unalienable Rights, that among these are Life, Liberty, and the Pursuit of Happiness,'* and I believe that the country where you are born; the money you have or do not have; or the color of your skin should not place you above or below other people."

"I concur with your assessment, Ms. Kae," said Thomas. "Your father indeed has a profound understanding of freedom, liberty, and human nature." Then to Adams: "I am committed, John. This paragraph condemning the slave trade should remain, even if it means insolvency for the Jefferson estate."

"I must confess," said Ben, "I wouldn't have been able to run the Pennsylvania Gazette without the help of George and King. And with Deborah gone, I don't know how I could get by in my Philadelphia home without Peter and Jemima."

"Neither Roger nor I have ever owned slaves," said Adams. "And Thomas is right, the sale of humans into a lifetime of servitude *is* a cruel war against human nature."

Topher couldn't believe Ben Franklin owned slaves.

"I don't say this often, John, but you are right," said Ben. "This is a bold statement to put in the declaration because the freedom from Great Britain and freedom for those without it should be its most enduring principles."

Roger raised his teacup and said, "Well stated, Dr. Franklin. I propose a toast."

"Roger, if I may," said Ben as he raised a glass of wine. "We are the wordsmiths, but the defense of our independence falls on the Continental Army; therefore, I propose a toast to General George Washington."

Everyone but Topher, Kae, and Fumnaya joined in.

Thomas said, "Let's move on to the next paragraph regarding the tyranny of King George."

Topher felt a tap at his elbow. It was Saimon and Matija.

Saimon whispered, "We need you in the physical therapy room."

"Anything's gotta be better than this," said Topher.

He was halfway there when Topher realized he never got an espresso.

In the boardroom turned physical therapy studio, another committee of five assembled for a different purpose. Here, the leader was Jaime Trueno, a National Park Service ranger. Others present were his twin brother, Juan; Matija, the techie of the group; and Saimon, the former special forces soldier. Topher completed the quintet.

"Topher, thanks for coming," said Jaime.

"What's going on?"

"Enough of the small talk," said Matija. "I analyzed the iPad pictures of the guys in the sports car and verified they *are* Phineas and Corbin, known Brokers of the Count throughout the Succession Prerogative."

Jaime said, "We've been tracking them for the past three days. We have spotted them all around Independence Mall, the Philadelphia Gold Exchange, and Declaration House."

Matija said, "I believe these younger iterations of Phineas and Corbin may not be as dangerous."

Saimon asked, "Why?"

"Because they haven't done the Civil War yet."

"How's that possible?" Jaime asked.

"I ran the pics through software Topher helped me refactor, and it calculated their age to be five to seven years younger than their 1863 morgue photos."

"That gives us an advantage," said Jaime.

"It also means we're meeting each other out of order," said Saimon. "It took four years and twelve Regents to defeat and kill eleven of the twelve known Brokers, and now we're fighting them again, only younger?"

Topher said, "I'm not sure which sounds crazier, the conversation in here or the one in the kitchen. And I'm not sure I belong in either of 'em."

"Not true," said Jaime. "We need you to be our eyes and ears when we escort the Committee of Five back to Independence Hall tomorrow afternoon when we send them back to 1776."

"Ben isn't healthy enough to go back," said Topher.

Saimon said, "I've been doing physical therapy with him every day. He can walk, but he'll need help up the stairs."

"I still don't get it," said Topher. "We know exactly where Phineas and Corbin are in Philadelphia, so what's the danger?"

Michael entered the room wearing his National Park Service uniform and set a large container on the therapy table. The jar was the same size as a bottle of soda, but half as tall. It had a wide, flat lid with a brass ball topping it. It looked identical to the one Juan had removed from the Franklin Cage when the Founders arrived nearly two weeks ago.

"What's that thing? I'm guessing it's not for booze."

Matija said, "It's a prototype terrestrial current device, one of four in existence. It's capable of harnessing and generating over a terawatt of energy from the Earth's ionosphere. This one is specifically calibrated to the Schumann resonance and tuned to Franklin's grounded cage in the bell tower."

"That makes *total* sense," said Topher.

Saimon said, "It's also from the future and the thing that makes time travel possible, but only in year increments, and only if the portal exists in the destination year."

"Thus the reason for the egg timer test," Matija added.

"Then why's it look old, not futuristic?"

"The inventor designed it to resemble a Leyden jar, and it wasn't for time travel. Its primary purpose is the wireless transmission of electricity for—"

"We all know this," Michael cut off Matija. "The more urgent matter is the Brokers are in 1776, and they used our backup Leyden seven days ago."

Saimon puffed up and approached Michael aggressively. "They stole it, and you've known about this an entire *week*? You're worse than Madame Zaphon."

Although less than a foot shorter and more than a hundred pounds lighter, Saimon didn't seem intimidated by Michael's far superior size and muscles.

Matija, dressed in a tailored lavender dress and black, shiny heels, stepped between the two men and separated them. "Testosterone won't provide any intelligent answers. Michael, to what year did it arrive a week ago?"

"2011," said Michael. "Right under our noses."

The room became as silent as a hospice for a long minute.

Topher said, "So someone stole your jawn, and we need to get it back from those morons in the orange sports car. "

Matija said, "That *jawn* is our Leyden jar, a backup calibrated to work above Independence Hall, and the Brokers somehow found it in 1776 and used it. They've always had one, but now they have two of the four prototypes. Luckily, I have an old GPS program to find it." She reached into her Chanel handbag, removed a rose gold flash drive, and gave it to Topher. "Inject this algorithm in the code you're refining for the security system, and that Leyden jar's location will light up like a spotlight in a field of fireflies."

Jaime stood at the window with a view of Independence Hall below and said, "If that signal comes anywhere near the mall from the time we escort them out of this building and into the bell tower, you need to alert everyone. That's your job, Topher."

"What does it mean if I get a hit?"

Michael said, "Danger, because if those younger versions of the Brokers come at us, they can't be killed."

CHAPTER TWENTY-TWO

TOPHER WHITE

INDEPENDENCE HALL INJUSTICE

Injustice in the end produces independence. -
Voltaire (From: *Tancrede* - Act III, 1761)

Outside Curtis Building - 6th & Sansom Street - Philadelphia, PA - Monday, June 27th, 2011 - 10:15 p.m.

In a microsecond, Topher White's heart felt like someone had yanked it into his throat. He saw the glint of light shining from a long blade displayed on the black-and-white video feed, followed by Jaime Trueno's head toppling from his shoulders before his body crumpled. After that, the screen only showed blood dripping from what looked like a sword. Topher couldn't see the face of the weapon's wielder to run the FRA, only the top of the hand, which displayed an intricate tattoo of a snake's head. Topher thought, *Did that really just happen? And who could have evaded all my software mods?* He switched to the tower staircase cam and saw four founders at the top with Saimon and Juan, but Ben was still at the bottom of the flight under the large window with Matija.

Despite the shock, Topher could only say, "Watch out!"

"What is it?" said Matija over the comm. "Phineas and Corbin?"

"No, someone with a long knife or machete."

"How far out?"

"Beneath you. Inside the building!"

Topher snapped the laptop shut and popped out of the back of the ambulance parked on 6th and Sansom Street.

He sprinted to Independence Hall and ran so fast it burned his lungs.

Over the earpiece, Saimon said, "Michael, find and neutralize the threat. Topher, stay at your post."

"Too late." Topher gasped before he swiped the door to the Supreme Court Room. Once inside, he descended the brief steps and sped across the historic chamber while thoughts of Ben Franklin split into packets across his brain that wouldn't reassemble into any logical outcome. What if any of the committee died in 2011 before getting sent back to 1776? Would America crumble and change instantaneously? What if Ben never made it to the cage with the others? What if he didn't sign the Declaration?

As he passed the tables covered in green cloth, Topher realized his own life might be in danger. What if the killer was still in the Central Hall?

He collided with a large man in a green Park Service uniform. He looked up and saw it was Michael, the guy who looked like an 80-year-old Dave Bautista.

"Shhhh," Michael hissed into his index finger, which was covered in blood.

Topher looked at his hands and saw they were shaking.

Michael deactivated his comm and gestured for Topher to do the same. When they were both cut off from the team, he said, "Jaime is dead."

"Saw the video."

"You see who did it?"

"Just the weapon."

"You shouldn't be here. I don't know where the assassin went. And if you would have stayed at your post, you could've—"

"He could've killed Ben and—"

"Be quiet and don't look down." Michael grabbed Topher's arm and pulled him through Central Hall into the Tower Stair Hall. They ascended the first flight of stairs and Topher was relieved to see Ben sitting under the sill below the large arched windows on the first landing. He was out of breath and pale. Matija was crouched next to him in a catcher's pose and seemed ready to spring up at any moment.

Michael activated his earpiece and said to Matija, "Come on. Juan is in the bell tower preparing the time portal with Saimon. He's going to make the trip with them in case there's danger on the other side."

Matija said, "But he's not —"

Michael cut her off and said, "Compartmentalize. We're not out of this yet. Now go help Saimon."

"Yes, sir."

She bounded up the stairs.

Topher said, "How're you gonna cram Juan's bulk in that cage with—"

"Get Dr. Franklin into the bell tower, Topher," said Michael. "I'm going down to neutralize the threat."

Topher said, "I'm not strong enough to help Ben if."

Michael was down the stairs before Topher could finish.

He cradled Ben's arm and said, "Let's get you back to 1776."

"My spirit is willing, but I'm afraid the flesh is weak."

CHAPTER TWENTY-THREE

SAIMON KHNKHLẬNG

THE WAR IS NOT YET OVER

สงครามยังไม่จบ อย่าเพิ่งนับศพทหาร
*Thai Proverb: sohng khraam yang mai johp
yaa pheerng nap sohp tha haan*

*Translation: The war is not yet over; don't
gloat over your enemy's body count.*

**Independence Hall - 520 Chestnut
Street - Philadelphia, PA - Monday,
June 27th, 2011 - 10:25 p.m.**

S aimon heard a scuffle behind the entrance door
to the bell tower on level two, but only Juan was

supposed to be inside. He believed the danger was downstairs, with Michael in pursuit.

Matija clustered the four grumbling Founders in the hall outside the Long Room. They wore the same clothes they as when they arrived over two weeks ago on June 11th. Out of breath, she whispered to Saimon, "Why the hesitation?"

Saimon addressed the comm, "Juan, you okay? All clear?"

Silence.

"Juan, come in."

No response.

Saimon put his ear to the door and held up a hand to command silence.

"I'll shelter them in the Long room." Matija then escorted the Founders away.

Saimon got out his Samsung Galaxy S II and opened the video feed app, but no signal. He backed away from the door and said, "Topher, I need eyes in the bell tower. Juan is non-responsive."

It took a long moment before Topher responded with, "Something's wrong. Cams are offline."

"How long?"

Topher stuttered, "Around the same time I, ah."

"—Same time you did what?"

"Left the ambulance and rushed over here."

Saimon swore in Thai, unholstered his weapon, and mumbled, "Guess I'm going in blind."

He creaked the door open, but didn't see Phineas and Corbin as expected. It was another pair of Brokers, enemies he fought in the 1860s: Astra, the

Athens Minx, and Marquis, the Paris Sadist. They had died in the Second Battle of Bull Run. Saimon saw their dead bodies, took their pictures in the makeshift morgue. But here they were: alive and dressed from top to bottom in black tactical gear with gas masks perched on their heads. Over at Franklin's cage, Juan wiped blood from his head as he struggled to stand upright. Saimon hoped Juan wasn't seriously injured because he was going to need that muscle.

Michael had said the Brokers couldn't die twice, but Saimon was going to challenge that theory.

They were making their egress and obviously hadn't perceived Saimon's entrance, so he announced, "Visiting hours are over, and that's not an authorized exit."

Marquis turned and froze with the Leyden jar held over his head while Astra's arms stretched through the window to receive it. Saimon figured they must have entered through the scaffolding that surrounded the bell tower during its renovations.

The Paris Sadist and Athens Minx looked like children caught stealing cookies.

Marquis the Frenchman slowly took one hand from the Leyden jar and pulled down the gas mask. Its night vision goggles lit up with demon-red pupils. He then reached for a small canister strapped to his chest. Saimon knew the shape but guessed at its contents: a flash-bang or incapacitating agent.

Saimon pulled the hammer back and said, "Touch that and I'll end you."

"Don't. He'll drop it," Juan said from behind.

Astra, the Greek seductress, said to Saimon with a wink, "I love a man with a big gun, short stuff, but I *must* add this to my collection."

She then moved to grab the Leyden jar.

Without warning, Juan charged at Marquis, but bumped Saimon, which caused him to pull the trigger. The shot grazed Marquis' ribcage, just below the armpit. Marquis grunted in pain and lost the grip of the Leyden jar. Astra lunged to snatch it, but only forced the front part of her body through the window. Juan used his forward momentum to twist onto his back and catch it over his chest. Juan cradled it, rolled over, and stumbled back to Franklin's cage. He looked like a drunken running back who had just retrieved a game-winning fumble.

Adrenaline could enhance judgment as well as impair it, which Saimon thought was the case when Marquis threatened to open the gas canister.

"Mask won't do you any good, Marquis. I can hold my breath for five minutes," said Saimon.

"How do you know my name?"

Astra screamed at Marquis, "Pop the pin, sissy boy!"

Saimon pivoted, aimed the gun at Astra's head, and pulled the trigger.

Nothing happened. His focus narrowed to the ejection port and saw it stovepiped.

For the first time, Saimon's reliable Colt .45 M1911 had jammed.

CHAPTER TWENTY-FOUR
TOPHER WHITE

BEN'S GOUTY KNEE

Be temperate in wine, in eating, girls, and sloth; Or the Gout will seize you and plague you both. - Benjamin Franklin (From *Poor Richard's Almanack* – October 30th, 1733)

Independence Hall - 520 Chestnut Street - Philadelphia, PA - Monday, June 27th, 2011 - 10:25 p.m.

Topher wasn't strong enough to support a weakened Ben Franklin up the hard wooden stairs. When he heard the shot fired from the bell tower, Topher lost his grip and Ben's bad knee hit the nose of the step, causing him to wince in pain, then crumple.

Michael said over the comm, "Heard a shot fired. Check in."

Motionless, Topher and Ben sat on the stairs for thirty tense seconds before Saimon said breathlessly, "It was me. Shot a Broker. We're fine, no casualties. Portal is secure."

Michael asked, "What happened?"

"They breached the bell tower through the scaffolding. Ones we didn't expect — the Minx and the Sadist."

"Which one did you hit?"

"Marquis. Both escaped after he sucker-punched me. Lights out for a minute. Juan was busy prepping —"

A power surge dimmed the lights, and Michael said, "Egg timer test must've started. Get Juan and the founders into the cage. As soon as you get a positive round trip, hit the plunger. With shots fired, you've got less than five minutes. I can hold off the Park Service, but not Philly PD."

"Ben's hurt," said Topher. "We're on the stairs."

"I'm coming to you, Topher," said Michael.

"That invention in your ear is fascinating," Ben grunted.

Topher saw sweat forming on Ben's forehead and tried to get him standing. "Slicker than the iPhone, ain't it?"

"I'm a useless old man right now. I fell on my gouty knee."

"It's all right. Someone much stronger will get you up these stairs and back to your time."

The power surged again as Michael bounced up the stairs to meet them. He carried a large, black case with the word PELICAN on it.

Over the comm, Topher heard Matija say, "Egg fully intact. Loading them in."

"Help me get Ben up there," Topher pleaded with Michael. "They're getting ready to leave."

Michael looked up the stairwell, then leveled his dark brown eyes and said, "We don't have time."

"What do you mean? You could carry him on your back."

Michael turned off the comm, then said to Topher, "I could, but whoever killed Jaime hasn't been located and we need Juan focused."

Ben said, "Mr. Jaime is dead?"

"I'm afraid so, Dr. Franklin," said Michael. "And there's not enough space in the portal."

"Ready to go," Matija said over the comm.

Michael reactivated the comm. "Send them Matija, but tell Juan it's a boomerang return. We need that Leyden jar back."

"We'll strand the Regents in 1776," said Matija.

Topher said, "You can't!"

Michael said, "Plunge it."

"But what about history?" said Topher. "The vote for independence and the declaration ending slavery. Ben *has* to be there for that."

A hum vibrated across the building, a sound Topher remembered from the day they arrived.

"Dr. Franklin didn't write it; Thomas Jefferson did," said Michael.

"Madame Zaphon wouldn't approve of—"

"I'm in charge," Michael shouted above the jet-engine noise rising over their heads. "And Madame Zaphon insisted on the Hamilton Plan in case things went sideways."

"It's not right to—"

The stairs shook, and the rumble reached its crescendo, vanquishing Topher's attempted diatribe. A crack reverberated across the building and extinguished the power. Through the tall window, Topher could only make out the shadow of the Penn Mutual building above the trees across Independence Square. Down at street level, the only visible lights were the flashing blue and red of the Philadelphia Police and Fire Department vehicles.

Topher turned back to the stairs. A descending pair of red eyes frightened him. Michael shielded Ben and Topher. The emergency lights came up, revealing Saimon in a gas mask with night vision goggles.

He peeled them off and said, "They got away safely, but we need to extract Dr. Franklin ASAP." Saimon held out a small canister with a pin at the top.

"What's that?" asked Topher.

"It's worse than tear gas," said Saimon.

Michael said, "Good. It'll give us the time we need. Nobody will breach if I tell them it went off."

Saimon said, "Seen this same kind back in Iran. Wait." He pointed at Michael's bloody hand print on Topher's shirt. "Is that blood?"

"Jaime is dead," said Michael.

"Tell me you caught the Broker who did it."

"Escaped. Don't know how."

The sirens outside multiplied with each passing moment, and Topher stared at the floor in guilt. If the security software had been better, maybe Jaime wouldn't be dead.

"This is going federal in no time flat," said Michael. "Homeland Security, FBI, NSA, everyone with a bad suit and a badge. As of now, I'm decommissioning the bell tower portal."

Topher said, "If this place gets locked down, how's Ben getting back in time to sign the Declaration?"

Michael handed the Pelican case to Saimon and said, "With this."

Saimon scoffed. "The Treasury Building Leyden jar? It only gives us a range to 1855."

An energy surge flickered the emergency lights.

Michael said over the comm, "Matija, bring down the Leyden jar that just arrived in the Franklin cage."

"Next stop is D.C. with Dr. Franklin, right?" asked Saimon.

"Not for him—just you and Matija. Dr. Franklin's bioelectromagnetics can't handle two jumps. He must go back in one."

Matija ran down the staircase with a Leyden jar cradled in her arms. "We're going to do another bootstrap?"

Michael said, "Yes, but this one's trickier. That's why you and Saimon need to get Tesla along the way."

"You can't be serious," said Saimon.

"That's rhetorical," said Matija. "Michael is *always* serious. Right, big guy?"

Michael seemed to ignore that and said, "I'll use this gas can as a distraction so you can load Dr. Franklin and yourselves into an ambulance. We'll rendezvous at the hangar."

Topher said, "Nobody answered my question."

Michael put his hand on Topher's shoulder. "With this portal out of commission, Dr. Franklin's only option is the Hamilton Plan."

Chapter Twenty-Five

TOPHER WHITE

The Hamilton Plan

Our virtues and our failings are inseparable, like force and matter. When they separate, man is no more. -Nikola Tesla (From *The Problem of Increasing Human Energy*, Century Illustrated Magazine - June 1900)

Prinus Ambulance Company - 428 N. American Street - Philadelphia, PA - Monday, June 27th, 2011 - 11:45 p.m.

I n the back of the ambulance, Topher White prepped an instant ice pack and placed it on Ben Franklin's knee. He looked forward into the cab and saw Independence Hall shrink in the rearview mirror as he processed tonight's disasters.

A brutal murder in Central Hall.

A shot fired in Tower Level 2.

Ben Franklin stuck in 2011.

All because his security hadn't caught the Brokers who breached Independence Hall at both ground level and through the bell tower's scaffolding. Topher couldn't delete Jaime's beheading video that ran through his mind on a loop. It made him nauseated. Why hadn't the software detected the swordsman's entrance, and how could he have evaded every camera inside?

"Cold without ice." Ben drew Topher's attention. "Another ingenious invention."

"Chemical reaction makes it work." Topher handed Ben another. "See—break it, and it turns frigid."

"Is there a libation in this carriage that could ease my pain?"

"Last time I drank alcohol, it was a Hennessy with my foster brother. His name is Todd."

"Would you pour me one?"

"An ambulance doesn't stock booze."

"Perhaps when we arrive at our destination."

The ambulance hit a pothole. Topher swore when his head hit the ceiling.

"I told you to strap in," Saimon shouted from the front compartment.

"Where are we going anyway?" asked Topher.

"Back to dispatch. We call it the hangar," Matija said from the driver's seat. "Michael and Madame

Zaphon believe our only option is the Hamilton Plan."

"We don't have time, and it's too risky," said Saimon. "How can we build a new portal and recalibrate this Leyden jar in five days?"

Matija scoffed. "She doesn't want to do it. Bet you a hundred bucks she'll box me out in favor of the other Croatian."

"Don't want to bet on anything right now," said Saimon. "We've already lost Jaime, and you and I know the psychopath responsible."

A video display lit up. Both its voice and image startled Topher.

"We need Nikola because we have three days to calibrate and test it," Madame Zaphon said from the screen.

"Who is that woman in the talking portrait?" Ben asked. "She has the most beautiful blue eyes I've ever seen."

"I'm Gabrielle Zaphon, Dr. Franklin. People call me Madame Zaphon. I apologize. We couldn't send you back to 1776 tonight."

"'Tis nothing, madame. Hardly the first time I've been late for an engagement."

"Unfortunately, we won't be able to use your Bell Lift Cage."

"Are we traveling to a new port?"

"We must build it first, Dr. Franklin."

"Please, call me Ben."

"Then you may call me Gabrielle. I'll have a snifter of cognac when you arrive, Ben."

Inside the cavernous garage of the Prinus Ambulance Company, Topher couldn't follow their arguments about someone named Nikola. The Independence Hall Leyden jar stood in the middle of a long, plastic folding table next to the Pelican case that cradled a twin Leyden jar nestled in foam. A long tube and a brown leather book stood next to the case. Ben sat in the back of a nearby ambulance and happily sipped an enormous glass of fancy brandy.

Saimon shouted above everyone, "Haven't we put him through enough?"

In a calm, even voice, Madame Zaphon said, "Mr. Tesla can make multiple time jumps with zero electrolyte destabilization. Much like all the Regents, Nikola has a unique body chemistry; electrical impulses don't affect him like they do for 99.8 percent of the population."

"Who's this Nikola, anyway?" Topher asked. "Another time traveler or Regent or whatever?"

"He is an adjunct member, much like you," said Madame Zaphon.

"Whatever it is, I'm sure Matija and I can figure it out," said Topher.

"There will be a time you and she will be perfectly capable, Mr. White. But not today. We need Mr. Tesla to stand up the Hamilton portal in Lower Manhattan within the next five days so we can send Ben back to 1776."

"So that's where we'll find Nikola, New York?" Topher asked.

"Yes, he is in New York City, but not in 2011." Madame Zaphon lifted the leather-bound book and flipped through it. Nobody spoke while she did this, and Topher noticed the pages weren't paper but thin, flexible computer screens. She swiped at it for a half minute and said, "1901 is the dial-in year because construction of the U.S. Custom House and Bowling Green subway station is underway. Jerneja and Filip have an office at the top floor of the Washington Building overlooking both projects in that year, so they'll have access to . . ."

While she droned on about construction sites and the Regents assigned to watch over Nikola Tesla, Topher scanned his mind, found his name in a science book, and skimmed it. He immigrated from Croatia and became a prolific inventor who experimented with radio waves and designed the alternating current electrical system. Like himself, Tesla had a photographic memory.

Topher interrupted Madame Zaphon's briefing with the obvious question: "If he's not from this time, how do we get him, and how does he send Ben back to 1776?"

Matija pointed at the Leyden jar in the military case and said, "We calibrated this one for the time portal in D.C. under the Treasury Building."

Topher said, "You have another time cage? Then it's easy. Let's go up to Washington and send Ben back with that one."

"Won't work," said Matija. "That time portal and building didn't exist in 1776."

"Can only go back as far as 1855 when we built it," said Saimon. "But we'll use it to arrive in Washington, 1901."

"Will we meet General Washington?" Ben asked.

"I still don't follow," said Topher. "Ben needs to get back to 1776, not 1901."

Madame Zaphon snapped the book shut and said, "Mr. Tesla's calculations make time travel possible." She pointed at the Leyden jar on the table. "He's the only one who can quickly recalibrate this Independence Hall device to a new Faraday cage. It's most ideal location is under the Alexander Hamilton U.S. Custom House."

Saimon scoffed and said, "The far-fetched Hamilton Plan."

"Let me do it," said Topher. "I've designed and written metric tons of complicated algorithms."

Matija asked, "What's your working knowledge of dynamical systems and differential equations?"

"I can pick it up fast," said Topher. Then to Madame Zaphon: "Please, if this is something technical, let me help." As soon as he said it, Topher realized he sounded as desperate as he felt. He thought that if he dove into this challenge and succeed, it would be a welcome distraction, something to assuage his guilt over his role in Jaime's death.

Madame Zaphon said, "With limited technology and an unworldly understanding of mathematics, Nikola came extremely close to inventing both terrestrial current and time travel in the early twentieth century. All without graphene, semiconductors, or computers."

"So, he's a genius with math," said Topher. "But what about time travel? How do you get from 1900 to 1776?"

"We go to 1901," said Matija. "And it requires two jumps in two separate portals. First, Saimon and I go to 1901 Washington, then take an express train to New York and retrieve Nikola Tesla. We take him to Philadelphia and dial-in the second trip to 1776 in Franklin's cage. Once there, we take an express coach, no trains in 1776, back to New York City where Nikola will have to recalibrate it for the new time portal built thirty feet under a military fort."

"Sounds too complicated." Topher pointed at the Leyden jars. "If these can only jump in year increments, why don't we wait until next year and send Ben back to 1776 from 2012 using the bell tower's cage? We could time it so he arrives shortly after we sent the others back tonight."

"I don't mind staying another year. The indoor necessaries are much better here than in my Philadelphia." Ben smiled and tossed back the remaining cognac.

Madame Zaphon said, "Not acceptable."

"Why?"

"Because the longer we keep someone displaced, the higher the risk of temporal delirium."

"What's that mean?"

Madame Zaphon said, "I selected the Regents not only for their skills, but their unique bioelectromagnetics. Saimon and Matija can handle multiple portal trips. For most, like Ben here, an extended furlough outside one's own time period can impair that person's ability to function upon return."

Topher said, "How long a furlough, and what happens?"

Saimon said to Topher, "It messes with your head if you're away too long."

"Not always," said Matija. "With the other historicals we've displaced, time delirium faded away and they readjusted."

"Or it doesn't go away," said Saimon. "Like with Tesla. We kept him almost a year while he calibrated the Treasury Building portal in 1855 and we cut it too close. Came within two weeks of his conception date and nearly Wolfi-Pauli ripped him. I believe that left permanent damage. Imagine the inventions he could have brought the world if Tesla's temporal delirium hadn't turned into temporal dementia."

Topher said, "A paragraph from a book I just recalled described this Tesla guy as a mad scientist, a germaphobe insomniac obsessed with the number three. He relates better to pigeons than people."

Madame Zaphon sighed and looked at Saimon. "I'm afraid we may have contributed to Nikola's madness, which is exactly why we cannot keep Ben in the early twenty-first another year. His intellectual fitness must be in its prime when he goes to France in October 1776."

"I've heard the Paris cuisine is much better than London," said Ben.

"He also needs to sign the Declaration of Independence before that," said Topher. "If he can't stay a year, why not have Saimon and Matija take Ben to the time portal in the Treasury Building, travel back to a safe year, then use the bell tower cage and return him to 1776? No new hardware, recalibration or mad scientist required."

Madame Zaphon said, "Two jumps in that short a period would cause Ben physical damage, and the surgery already compromised his health."

Topher scoffed. "So, our only option to get Ben back to 1776 is an unstable genius?"

"I've studied the algorithms from both Leyden jars," said Matija. "But we configured them to work over dirt, not schist."

Topher said, "Say what?"

"I said *schist*, not the word you thought I said. Below and above Manhattan are bedrock called schist. Great for skyscrapers, but a unique challenge for the recalibration of this Leyden jar because of its conductivity."

In the leather-bound book, Madame Zaphon flipped to a 1776 map of Lower Manhattan. The page highlighted a square building with arrowheads on each corner and labeled "Fort George." She tapped the northwest tip and said, "Thirty feet under this bastion is where we must build it. Recruit resources only from St. John's Masonic Lodge. They'll ensure every available laborer, blacksmith, and stonemason works around the clock to dig the hole and construct the time portal."

"What'll they think it is?" Saimon asked.

Madame Zaphon set the book down, popped open the end of the tube, and spilled its contents onto the table. "This schematic is for a prison cell. They'll think it's a dungeon."

Saimon asked, "But if we're bootstrapping this new cage, how do we make sure it isn't dug up or destroyed when they're building the U.S. Custom House or Bowling Green subway station at the turn of the twentieth?"

Madame Zaphon flattened the schematics across the table.

"What's bootstrapping?" Topher asked.

"It's when you build something in the past, and it appears in the present," said Saimon.

"But we must place it where it is both secured and won't be disturbed for decades," said Matija as she hovered over the drawings. "This one specifies an iron floor with granite walls and ceiling and to surround the iron cell."

Madame Zaphon turned to the next sheet and said, "Here are Mr. Gilbert's plans for the foundation of the U.S. Custom House. During the excavation at this northwest corner, they shall find the portal, but it will have Lenape carvings on the door. Experts will determine it to be an ancient tomb of an important Indian chief, and people in that time are very superstitious. These gold coins will purchase the silence of the stonemasons in who will faithfully carve this deception. The masons are very good at keeping secrets."

"I am a Freemason, Gabrielle," said Ben. "Good chaps. Tell them they're building it for me, and you'll have their fealty."

"They'll be in it for the money," said Topher. He looked at the map in the open book and saw blinking yellow lights on Staten Island. "What's that mean?"

"Another bit of motivation," said Madame Zaphon.

"That's where the British armada lands in five days on July 3rd, 1776," said Saimon. "In six weeks, there'll be over thirty-two thousand troops in four hundred ships surrounding New York City."

Madame Zaphon added, "And by August 27th, Washington's army will retreat from New York City, which means the portal in Fort George will no longer be available for use."

Topher said, "So there's a small window to build and use it? This keeps getting more insane by the minute. Why not build it somewhere else in Philadelphia?"

"We need to ensure the site is not disturbed, destroyed, or changed in 1776, 1901, and 2011. Mr. Lamb has studied and fully vetted this location, but he is not available. The land is within the acceptable range of the Schumann resonance," said Madame Zaphon. "And our current situation meets the criteria set for such a set of circumstances."

Saimon said, "That's why we build portals in preserved and protected historic places, like Fort

Sumter, the Treasury Building and Independence Hall."

"And now you're going to build one next to a subway," said Topher. "Not exactly historic."

"It will also put us in a better position to avenge Jaime's murder," said Saimon.

"You're not to tell Juan his brother is dead when you arrive in 1776," said Madame Zaphon.

"Why?"

"Everyone needs to stay on mission," she said.

Topher saw her dark blue eyes fill with tears.

"Then what's my job?" Topher asked.

Her voice was shaky but firm. "The Park Service and FBI will question everyone who was near Independence Mall today."

"I deleted every bit of video. They won't find me on it."

"You can't erase the memories of eyewitnesses, so that's why you're leaving for New York tonight with Ben."

"Why? I know every abandoned tunnel, train station, and safe house across the city. I've been underground - that's how I stayed off the grid and evaded youse with all your technology. I can do the same for Ben."

"You don't know the Brokers," said Saimon. "After what happened tonight, you wouldn't be safe *anywhere* in Philadelphia."

CHAPTER TWENTY-SIX

GIOVANNI ROSSO

FRETTING CARES MAKE GREY HAIRS

But there is only one thing which gathers people into seditious commotion, and that is oppression.

- John Locke (October 3rd, 1689)

Cipriani Restaurant - 55 Wall Street - New York, NY - Tuesday, June 28th, 2011 - 7:35 a.m.

The morning's Wall Street Journal headline burnt Giovanni's while his breakfast cooled. It was: "NSA Closes Independence Hall After Security Breach." Two Brokers named Corbin and Phineas were supposed to have been observing the five founders in Philadelphia, but today's paper and Rex's absence over the past two days suggested more than reconnaissance.

He dialed Rex's number, but it went straight to voice mail. He left a message: "Something happened in Philadelphia, and I demand assurance you had nothing to do with it. I'm at the Cipriani Club for my —"

"Plain oatmeal," Rex answered with a thud of his walking stick to announce his arrival. He appeared haggard and didn't remove the dark-tinted Wayfarer sunglasses as he grumbled, "With a net worth of twenty-three billion dollars, you could afford some blueberries to go with it, Herr Rosso."

"It keeps my system clean and my mind focused." Giovanni held a shiny, unused spoon to his face and admired his reflection. "It keeps me ageless, see? I don't appear older than forty-six. The magazines and newspapers love doing photo shoots. They always ask what products I use. If only they knew the truth."

"Then why not live it up? How about some bacon? Better yet, a bloody steak and scrambled eggs."

Giovanni heard the evasion in his voice, but was more disturbed by what he thought might be blood splatter on the shiny black lapel of Rex's suit coat.

"How long before this all gets traced back to me?" Giovanni pointed at the dark red stain.

"What?"

"Blood and money always leave trails to its heir."

"Not always," said Rex, who remained standing.

"All it takes is someone clever enough to follow it, and our time here is finished."

"You sound paranoid."

Giovanni held up the front page of the newspaper and said, "Today's paper justifies my feeling."

Rex waved to the lone server on the other side of the empty restaurant. He then tried to adjust a tie that wasn't there—another anomaly. Between that and the sunglasses, Giovanni knew Rex Purson was guilty. He then noticed the backside of a curvy woman with long, curly, dark hair near the hostess stand. She wore a perfectly tailored magenta dress and shiny black heels. It was the most pleasurable thing he had seen that morning until she turned around to see it was Astra Barakel, one who wielded feminine wiles more skillfully than Rex did a sword—and often more deadly.

Giovanni nodded in Astra's direction. "Why'd you bring the courtesan?"

"She has skills above the waistline, Herr Rosso," said Rex, who then ordered a quadruple espresso when the server arrived. "Did you know she has a PhD in astronomy and taught at the National Technical University of Athens before I recruited her into the Brokers?"

"I didn't summon you for her CV."

"She and Marquis were at Independence Hall last night with me."

"I didn't allow that, and why isn't he here?"

"Astra was with him and can explain."

Giovanni folded the newspaper under his arm and stood. "Not here—in my office."

"Ja, Herr Rosso. Leo is on the curb with the Mercedes running."

Giovanni Rosso's Office – 40 Wall Street, 75th Floor - New York, NY – Tuesday, June 28th, 2011 - 8:05 a.m.

His trading theater was the most extravagant, indulgent command center on Wall Street, perhaps the world. The focal point of the room was a near-replica of the eighteenth century Comédie-Française. It had a stage three feet high, framed with eighteenth-century inspired French woodcarvings of cherubim and leaves covered in 24 karat gold flake. Hand-carved crown molding adorned the space between the wall and the curve to the ceiling, which was painted sky blue and dotted with clouds so realistic they seemed to move. Mounted on the back of the stage was an array of eight high-resolution LED monitors, each an impressive seventy inches that were flanked by crimson velvet stage curtains. They opened automatically when Giovanni, Rex, and Astra entered the room. Giovanni walked the few steps into the custom-built dark Mozambique wood balcony at the back of the room, which faced screens scrolling a constant stream of market information from around the world. Twelve Italian leather swivel chairs filled the auditorium section, where Rex and Astra found seats closest to the stage, far as possible from their boss.

"Out with it," said Giovanni. "Spare no details."

The account Rex and Astra told of the events inside Independence Hall validated his concerns. It wasn't paranoia after he learned there was physical evidence. They would discover blood from Marquis Amon both in the bell tower and down the scaffolding where he had escaped. The worst part was how Rex justified the beheading of a Park Service ranger. Throughout the entire explanation, Giovanni couldn't divert his eyes from the dried blood strewn across Rex's coat and shirt like the first stroke on a macabre Jackson Pollock canvas.

For the first time in years, Giovanni didn't have a quick-witted response.

"Herr Rosso, say something," said Rex.

Giovanni slumped his shoulders and exhaled. "It's going to happen all over again. We almost made it twenty years without an incident, even after our success with changing history in the twentieth century. But your shortcut in trying to assassinate the American founders has put my entire enterprise at risk. All because this country is *verurteilt*, as you always say."

"It *is* doomed," Rex said as he slowly walked around the chairs toward Giovanni. "Starts in 2016, and gets much after that."

"What about the present? Soon it will be the FBI, Homeland Security, and the NSA pursuing me, not the British crown trying to lock me up in the Tower of London. Here's an idea. Let's shut down here, go to Germany, and use the time portal to steal the crown jewels."

"You have enough money to make a dozen exact replicas," said Rex.

"But what's the fun in that? I'd fancy the originals."

Rex said, "The media is calling the incident at Independence Hall a break-in, just like they did when the Brokers did Watergate. Nothing mentioned about the dead or injured in the story back then, and I doubt they'll report any deaths from yesterday."

"How many did you kill?" Giovanni pointed at Rex's shirt.

"*Es spielt keine Rolle,*" said Rex, which infuriated Giovanni because he always said that German phrase to make the important sound innocuous.

"It matters if I take the blame for what happened in Philadelphia. I'll not go down like Nixon and his cronies."

Rex raised his hands in surrender. "I've told you before, no one can link me or any of the Brokers to you or the companies you own because they've never been on your payroll. They're always compensated in cash or untraceable gold coins. According to all your bookkeeping, computer records, and even security cameras, I don't exist and neither do the Brokers. *Sorge macht vor Zeiten grau.*"

"I'm not worrying," said Giovanni. "And my hair remains perfectly black. How can you be sure there isn't a photo, video, or record of you or any of the other Brokers?"

Rex said, "Jack Chazaqiel spent the last five hours electronically searching Philadelphia for any trace of our existence, both public and private, and hasn't found a thing. That's outside the normal, daily search-and-destroy programs he uses for any image, file, or public video of the Brokers in the twenty-first century."

"It's not the machines or systems that are prone to failure, but the humans who create them," said Giovanni. "That's enough, Rex. I'm done with the Brokers. All my instincts tell me to disband and go back to Europe."

Rex moved so close into Giovanni's personal space, he could smell the cigarettes on his breath. "We cannot stop when we've barely begun."

Giovanni stepped back, straightened the lapels of his jacket and pronounced, "The plan was to use the time portal to stop America before it could separate from Great Britain. The founders escaped 2011 and went back to 1776, where the Declaration of Independence still happens. But it failed because you didn't have my input or approval on tactics."

"*Ja*, Herr Rosso, but we still have one of their Leyden jars. And almost got another that would have guaranteed success. Perhaps you *were* right—It was a bold plan, maybe hasty."

"As usual—that's why you need me," said Giovanni.

"*Ja*, Herro Rosso," said Rex. "What do you propose for tactics?"

"Since Astra and Marquis failed in 1776, we'll stop this country from declaring independence with an overpowering military, not targeted assassinations."

"You never told us the founders had time-traveling protectors," said Astra.

Giovanni pointed at her and said, "And you haven't earned an opinion, succubus." Then to Rex: "How many can we send to 1775?"

Rex counted on his fingers and said, "Half of the Brokers — Corbin Raum and Phineas Ophis, the demolitions expert and the weapons dealer. Then there's Mavis Camio and Rocco Bobel, the negotiator and the nerve agent scientist. Last pair safe to send to that time are Sol Shamsiel and Egon Azrael, the astronomer and the blacksmith."

"A motley set of skills, to be sure," said Giovanni. "Get the Gulfstream V prepped for departure."

Rex asked, "Destination is *Schloß* Louisenlund?"

"Kiel Airport this time," said Giovanni. Then to Astra: "Give the Leyden jar to Phineas Ophis. He will lead the delegation."

"As you wish, Mr. Rosso," Astra said with a slight curtsy.

Giovanni scoffed. "Spare me the false humility."

Astra seemed to ignore the slight and asked, "Will Phineas require the Leyden jar Marquis and I took from 1776?"

"No," said Giovanni. "We will use it to build a time portal right here in Manhattan."

Rex said, "Even if we arm them with future tech weapons, six people in 1775 are hardly an overpowering military."

"We need to wield the Brokers like scalpels, not chainsaws," said Giovanni. "I want Phineas and Mavis to meet with Prince Karl to negotiate the commission of a large German auxiliary from Hesse-Kassel. The English army and navy do not possess the brutality required to suppress the American revolutionaries, but they will."

"*Sehr gut*, Herr Rosso," Rex said with a smile. "My ancestors in *Deutschland* will take down America if King George the Third's army fails."

"Exactly," said Giovanni. "They will serve two purposes in the late eighteenth century. First, they will assist the soldiers from Hesse-Kassel with intelligence and military tactics. Their other goal is to find any of these time-traveling protectors, as Astra calls them, take their Leyden jar, and then kill them. I will not tolerate competition."

"Before you track them down, we should stop their ability to time jump and destroy the metal cage in the Philadelphia bell tower," said Astra.

Giovanni pointed his finger at her and said, "But there's something else you aren't telling me about last night when the founders escaped. I can sense it."

Rex said to Astra, "Go ahead, tell him what the time portal operator in the Independence Hall bell tower said before he shot Marquis."

Astra's eyes narrowed. "That cocky little *malaka* knew Marquis' name."

"How's that possible?" Giovanni asked.

"I grilled Marquis about it, and he swore they'd never met before," said Astra.

Rex said, "He's obviously a time traveler and Marquis hasn't met him yet."

"Agreed," said Giovanni. "That is why you and the others are going to destroy any remaining protectors in this century. Spare no expense. If I am to broker the failure of the American experiment, you must ensure I have a complete monopoly on time travel."

CHAPTER TWENTY-SEVEN

SAIMON KHNKHLạNG

BOOTSTRAPPING AN S.O.S.

*And I leave off as I began, that live or die,
survive or perish, I am for the Declaration.
It is my living sentiment, and by the blessing
of God it shall be my dying sentiment. Independence now, and Independence for ever*

- John Adams, Speech to the Continental Congress (July 1st, 1776)

Northwest Bastion of Fort George - 1 Bowling Green - New York, NY - Monday, July 1st, 1776 - 6:00 a.m.

Within two days of their arrival at Fort George on Manhattan's southern tip, a large team of laborers had already excavated a thirty foot deep hole under the northwest bastion of the fort. Four blacksmiths worked day and night to build a metal cage at the construction site. When asked, American soldiers were told that it was a new prison made especially for the Loyalist scourge on the Continental Army, led by Governor Tryon.

For Saimon, it was comforting to see his friend Thomas William Moedig, a fellow time-traveling Regent who went by the name of Billy Lee. Madame Zaphon had recruited Billy in the late 1800s while he was on tour with Buffalo Bill Cody. Anyone assigned to protect General Washington had to be an excellent horseman, and Billy Moedig was the best in any time period. His close connection to General Washington gave the prison construction project legitimacy, which allowed Saimon the leeway to get it done quickly.

During the building of the underground time portal, Tesla walked along the shoreline and developed the calculations necessary for time travel in his head. Saimon knew the scientist always perfected inventions mentally before committing them to paper. But this time, Matija insisted he verbalize the calculations daily so she could write them in a notebook. It helped that she spoke Croatian, and her motherly demeanor bent Tesla into compliance. It took three days for the numbers to trickle in, which was made slower because Tesla's obsessive-compulsive disorder drove him to walk around the circumference of the fort three times before descending into the portal's granite-walled room.

In the lamp-lit chamber, Saimon prepared the Leyden jar for reprogramming after Matija received the last section of the algorithm. He pressed a button on the cap of the leather blueprint tube that projected a computer screen onto the unpolished granite door carved with Lenape symbols. Matija arrived and tapped the calculations onto the virtual keyboard projected onto the table. Those calculations transferred wirelessly into the Leyden jar.

Matija completed the reconfiguration and declared it ready for the egg timer test. Saimon connected the copper grounding rod to the cage, placed an egg in the Leyden jar, and positioned it in the middle of the iron-bottomed floor. He scrolled the date to 2011, plunged the ball, and closed the iron door. Tesla, Matija, and Saimon peered into the cage, which rumbled with energy as the Leyden jar elevated three feet into the air. Ice crystals crawled across the newly forged iron bars. Within sixty seconds, the Leyden jar disappeared with a blast of cold air, extinguishing the oil lamps on the table and messing up Tesla's perfectly groomed black hair. Saimon lit up the room with a click of his stopwatch.

At four minutes, thirty seconds, the Leyden jar whooshed into existence midair before it slowly lowered, mocking gravity as if the air were a viscous fluid while it sunk to the iron floor and landed like a feather. Saimon opened the icy cage and removed the top of the Leyden jar. His body went from tense to limp when he saw the egg looked like it had exploded in a microwave oven. Either Matija had mistyped when re-coding the Leyden jar, or Tesla missed a variable.

The theory was that the concrete poured around the copper grounding rod was to blame. In their haste to get Ben Franklin back to 1776, neither Tesla nor Matija had considered how it could change their measurements of the Earth's resonance. Tesla insisted they collect new metrics every half hour, and by six that morning, he had revised the calculations.

Tesla proposed a two-stage test. The first was a round trip to 1901 and back, which was successful. Billy showed up with a large pot of coffee and fresh eggs for another test. After an all-niter, the caffeine was a welcome friend. Everyone partook except for Tesla, who wouldn't touch his teacup unless he had three cloth napkins with which to wipe it down.

After coffee, Saimon turned the numbers to 2011 on the Leyden jar and depressed the plunger.

The round trip took seven minutes when it should have been under five.

When it returned, Saimon anxiously retrieved the Leyden jar and, opening it, found the egg fully intact. No visible cracks in the shell. But when he grabbed it, the entire egg crumbled like meringue. It disappointed Saimon, but Tesla's reaction was unexpected. Perhaps it was his lack of sleep, pride in his abilities, obsessive-compulsive tendencies, or because multiple tests had failed, but Nikola Tesla, their most important asset in creating a new time portal fainted, crumpling to the ground as if someone cut the strings holding him up.

Saimon waved an open vial of ammonium carbonate under Tesla's nose, which shocked him back to consciousness. Unfortunately, he spoke Croatian so rapidly, Matija couldn't translate. Tesla's alertness lasted less than two minutes before he dropped back into a coma-like state. Saimon waved the chemical under Tesla's nostrils again, but there was no response.

Saimon took a deep, calming breath. "That sure went sideways."

"Perhaps he will come out of it," said Matija.

"I don't think so. The ammonium carbonate should have brought him around that second time."

"What do we do?" Billy asked.

"Stick to the priorities," said Saimon. "First, we need to ensure another Pennsylvania delegate covers Franklin's vote tomorrow. Billy, find Captain Hamilton and have him write a note on behalf of General Washington that explains Franklin's absence—make it health related—gout should be sufficient. If everything holds together, Alexander Hamilton will write a lot for Washington in the future. You'll be delivering that personally to the Continental Congress."

Matija said, "Excuse me?"

Saimon raised his hands in surrender and said, "Believe it or not, the Hamilton Plan covers this Tesla-being-incapacitated scenario."

Matija said, "Why can't I work on the calculations until Tesla regains consciousness and sends Billy to Philadelphia?"

"Not yet," said Saimon. "First, I need you to prep the Leyden jar data on a 21st century data stick."

Matija said, "Got it. Then what?"

"Samuel Fraunces' tavern on Pearl Street. I'm going to bootstrap an S.O.S to Madame Zaphon with that data."

CHAPTER TWENTY-EIGHT
TOPHER WHITE
UNLIKELY TOURISTS

Tonight, we gather to affirm the greatness of our nation — not because of the height of our skyscrapers, or the power of our military, or the size of our economy. Our pride is based on a very simple premise, summed up in a declaration made over two hundred years ago: "We hold these truths to be self-evident, that all men are created equal, that they are endowed by their Creator with certain inalienable rights, that among these are life, liberty and the pursuit of happiness." That is the true genius of America — a faith in simple dreams, an insistence on small miracles.
- Barack Obama, speech at the Democratic National Convention (July 27th, 2004)

International Mercantile Marine Company Building - 1 Broadway - New York, NY - Friday, July 1st, 2011 - 6:00 a.m.

New York seemed daunting after Madame Zaphon dropped Topher White and Ben Franklin off at the very expensive luxury apartment on the top floor of 1 Broadway in Lower Manhattan. She gave Topher a no-limit credit card and didn't put restrictions on their movements. He thought it would be house arrest again, like in Philly, but Topher figured the convoluted mission to build a new time portal in 1776 was more important to Madame Zaphon. Given this freedom, Topher concluded the best action was to explore the city with Ben Franklin at his employer's expense.

After imprinting the subway maps onto his mind, Manhattan became familiar in the four short days of sightseeing, dining, and discussing challenging topics. Topher knew that today, July 1st, 2011, was the last full day he and Ben would have together. If the Hamilton Plan was a success, Ben would travel back to 1776 so he could vote for American independence. And despite the arguments, disagreements, and adventures as tourists in the Big Apple, Topher realized he would miss Ben's presence, jokes, and occasional sage advice.

Through the penthouse window of the International Mercantile Marine Company Building, Topher stared down at the ornate Beaux-Arts building across the street, which was a U.S. Custom House when it opened in 1907, but today it housed the National Museum of the American Indian and the National Archives. Back in 1776, it was the site of a military structure called Fort George; that's where Saimon, Matija, and the inventor Nikola Tesla were building and configuring a new time portal. If they were successful, it would appear below ground and between the historic building and the Bowling Green Control House. The sudden apparition of an object in the present that was made or placed in the past is a phenomenon the Regents called bootstrapping.

Topher's phone buzzed, telling him the morning's breakfast delivery was downstairs.

"Has our meal arrived? I'm famished." Ben's voice came from behind him, startling Topher because he hadn't heard the approach. And he wouldn't repeat the mistake of turning around to look at him.

"No clothes, no food, old man."

"I do wish these windows would open. My body could use some fresh air to cleanse the mind and spirit."

"You walking around nude again?"

"Natural as the day I was born."

Averting his eyes, Topher picked up a pair of synthetic gray pants, flopped over a nearby chair, then threw them over his shoulder. "Today's the last day you get to wear these, so get dressed."

"I would like to bring them back."

"The world isn't ready to see you wearing elastic-waisted, synthetic slacks in 1776 *or* in 2011."

"What about the britches, or what you call underwear?"

"Not another word until you're fully clothed."

"Fine." Ben's tone was petulant. "Then what?"

"After breakfast, we're checking the subway again for the signal. If it's there, we'll know the bootstrap was a success. If it isn't, then we see more of the city."

The only thing more ridiculous than the polyester pants and the floral shirt was the bright red mobility scooter Ben used to get around the city. One benefit it provided was a fast pass into the New York Public Library and easy access to the subway, which helped them avoid crowds. They took the Bowling Green station elevator.

When the door opened, Topher headed toward the platform and heard a voice behind him. "Hey, old man, watch where you're going."

The angry passenger pointed at Ben, who held his hands up in surrender.

"Sorry about that," said Topher. "He's new to using this."

"Well, he just ran over my ingrown toenail," said the passenger.

"Apologies, madam," said Ben. "My knee is—"

"How can you assume my gender?" the passenger snapped.

Ben appeared puzzled at the retort.

Topher said, "We both apologized and gotta catch the next train."

"What are you, his caretaker or day-nanny?"

"You shouldn't *assume* anything about my relationship with this man," said Topher. "And if I told you who he is, you wouldn't believe it." Then to Ben: "Let's go to the four train."

On the way there, Ben asked, "Why do all these ports smell the same?"

"That subway scent is universal. It's like this in Philly, too."

"What's our destination after this? I'd fancy more time in the library."

"That was for my research. And we're not going anywhere until we're done here."

They strolled past every poster framed against the orange-tiled wall, and Topher scanned each one for the prearranged signal that the time portal was ready: an advertisement for a new exhibit at the National Museum of the American Indian titled The Lenape of Manhattan Island.

The frame where it was supposed to be was empty.

"I'm not sure if you're going back," said Topher.

Ben gestured to the stairs that led to the old Bowling Green Control House and said, "Not unless you can make this scooter fly."

"Not funny."

"What's wrong?"

"Madame Zaphon gave me two tasks. First, find the location of their stolen Leyden jar."

"You found it at the building site for the . . . What did you call it?"

"World Trade Center. Remember, I told you that when I was a kid, planes crashed into the original buildings."

"Quite tragic, yes."

"Twenty-six hundred people died there, and now they're putting up expensive buildings around their graves, all in the name of money and profit."

"Why would they put the time travel Leyden jar there?"

"Don't know, but my tweaks to Matija's software are solid. It's underground, but there's no way we can get past physical security to get it."

"What was the other task?"

"I told you to check that the portal's ready for your return to 1776."

"Is it right here, where you check this frame on the wall?

"No, but it's close." Topher pulled up a blueprint on his iPhone and showed it to Ben.

"Mr. Saimon called it a 'bootstrap'—how does that happen?"

"Honestly, I don't know how any of this works. But it ain't here yet."

"All in good time. He that can have patience can have what he will."

"You will not make it back to Philadelphia for the vote on independence if you don't leave today. What if the entire world changes overnight because you aren't there?"

"Shall we get a drink? I crave a rum punch."

"I told you, nobody serves alcohol for breakfast in New York. This ain't Las Vegas."

"If Las Vegas can get me a drink, that is where we shall go."

"If I took you there, you'd never want to leave."

"Then what do you propose?"

"Starbucks for espresso, then a boat ride. There's a French statue I'd like you to see."

Staten Island Ferry – Upper New York Bay - New York, NY – Friday, July 1st, 2011 – 10:04 a.m.

Topher and Ben leaned on the rails, staring at the Statue of Liberty in the distance while the boat crawled across the Upper Bay.

Ben must have sensed something was off, because he was more direct than usual.

"Why do you fret about things over which you have no control?"

Topher cocked his head to the side and said, "You think I'm worried?"

"I may be hard of sight, but I am hardly blind," said Ben.

Topher pointed at the Statue of Liberty and said, "I've been independent since I was nine years old. Escaped some serious abuse at the hands of someone who was supposed to protect me—foster parents, not birth parents—never knew them. Don't even know who they are. Only one who helped was my foster brother Todd when I was off the grid." He pulled down one sleeve of his compression shirt. "But I'm thinking about how you're responsible for the independence of the country I live in today—and feeling like I'm responsible if it all falls apart if you don't vote for it. Then you need to go to France. And they were so grateful, they gifted America that statue."

"I fail to understand your logic."

"The point is, if you're not sent back to 1776 today or tomorrow, maybe we'll wake up and there'll be a statue of Joseph Stalin in Lady Liberty's place."

Ben gently put his hand on Topher's shoulder and recoiled out of instinct. After a beat, he said, "My friend, you perceive this from a personal viewpoint, not one that is political."

"I don't know what you mean." Topher relaxed, looked into Ben's gray eyes, and noticed the tiny glasses weren't perched on his nose. "What's the difference?"

Ben said, "Let me tell you *my* story as a means of explanation. As a youth in Boston, I worked for my brother James. I was an indentured servant and helped print his newspaper, The New England Courant. It was a successful venture."

"Did you write for it?"

"Not officially. James forbade it. He did not believe a fifteen-year-old was capable, so I got published by writing as an old lady named Silence Dogood. After my early morning swim in Boston Harbor, I would handwrite these letters and slide them under the door of the print shop. He published them, and they helped sell a lot of newspapers."

"That's a stupid name. How'd your brother take it seriously?"

"It was a pseudonym, a pen name. Very common in my time. But the writing was quite good, and he needed to fill the paper."

"Online, a pseudonym is called a handle. I don't go by Topher—it's usually ZooS."

"Like the Greek god Zeus?"

"No—named after Konrad Zuse, an old, dead German who invented the first computer," said Topher. "Better than Silence Dogood."

Ben chuckled and said, "And I should have left it that way. It seems honesty is not always the best policy because when I told James it was I who wrote those letters, he became enraged. He berated and beat me for months after that. I couldn't take it any longer and felt my only option was to flee Boston. I was seventeen years old at that time—same as you. It was my first genuine act of personal independence. Like you, I escaped the abuse and used my God-given gifts to support myself."

"I feel you. Sorry that happened."

"It wasn't easy when I arrived in Philadelphia with a handful of farthings in my pocket, but I made friends, connections, and lots of mistakes. But what I'm trying to say is that independence and isolation aren't the same things. You need to associate with good people with a high work ethic like yourself to enhance your personal independence."

"I don't know where you're going with this," said Topher. The ferry was slowing down to dock at St. George Terminal on Staten Island.

"The point is simple. Political independence isn't the same as personal independence. The fate of a new nation shouldn't rest on the shoulders of one man—certainly not me. It is naïve to believe the fate of America is *that* fragile."

Topher's phone rang.

It was Madame Zaphon.

"I'm in the apartment." She sounded impatient. "Where are you and Ben?"

"Staten Island Ferry."

"Don't get on. You must meet me at Fraunces Tavern on Pearl Street. It's a short walk from where you are."

"We've already crossed."

"Then take the next boat back to Whitehall Terminal."

"Why so urgent?"

"Saimon bootstrapped a message from 1776."

"What's it say?"

"We'll find out after you dig it up."

CHAPTER TWENTY-NINE

TOPHER WHITE

FRAUNCES TAVERN

The truth is too simple: one must always get there by a complicated route. - Amantine-Lucile-Aurore Dupin, From a letter to Armand Barbès (May 12th, 1867)

Fraunces Tavern - 54 Pearl Street - New York, NY - Friday, July 1st, 2011 - 11:00 a.m.

Ben and Topher argued from the time they left Whitehall Terminal until they arrived at the corner of Pearl and Broad Street at the front steps into Fraunces Tavern.

"Why would I take you to the wrong place? Madame Zaphon texted me the address."

"I met Mr. Fraunces in New York," said Ben. "Impressive man, a true patriot, and a freed slave. Sam Fraunces is also a friend of General Washington."

"Wait a minute," said Topher. "Back in 1776, an African American owned this place?"

"He was African but not American. Nobody was then."

"What's your point?"

Ben gestured to the sign hanging in the building's corner. "Sam Fraunces did not put his name on the sign. His tavern was called the Queen's Head, and it was on Pearl Street."

"We *are* on Pearl Street, and this building looks really old. So this must be it."

"I've been there, and this does not resemble the Queen's Head."

"You've been to hundreds of taverns; how would you even remember?"

"Not everyone has a perfect memory like you, and we didn't have instant portraits back then."

"You mean pics," said Topher. "And I like you better when you're drinking."

A female voice emerged from behind. "The original tavern never had a whiskey bar—you must try it, Ben."

Topher spun around, startled to see Madame Zaphon. She wore the same straw hat and white pantsuit. Pinned to the lapel was a fresh Madonna lily.

"You can't sneak up on us like that," said Topher.

"Good morning, Ben and Topher," said Madame Zaphon.

"I would stand to greet you, Gabrielle, but my knee hasn't recovered from a recent bout with clumsiness," said Ben.

Topher helped Ben from the scooter and inside to a comfortable leather chair in the Dingle Whiskey Bar. Once they had settled and ordered drinks, Madame Zaphon gestured accusingly at Ben, but addressed Topher: "What on God's green Earth did you do to his hair?"

"I did nothing. We stopped at a fancy barber off Wall Street yesterday, but they don't do Afros, so they gave Ben this new style. It's an improvement, right?"

"He can't go back looking like that."

"I'll get him a hat or a wig. Nobody'll notice," said Topher. "I'm sure you didn't ask to meet us here to discuss fashion, so why'd you want to meet us here and not at the new portal site?"

Madame Zaphon lowered her eyes slightly. "Not everything has gone as planned."

Topher asked, "What happened?"

"We know they have bootstrapped the portal," said Madame Zaphon. "It appeared three days ago in the blink of an eye."

"What are we sitting around here, then? Let's send Ben back now."

"Saimon, Matija, and Tesla should have arrived as well. I suspect the egg timer tests failed," said Madame Zaphon.

"That takes us back to my first question."

"We are here because, according to the Hamilton Plan, if something goes wrong, they should send a message to the lower level of this building, which existed in 1776 *and* today." She removed a device from her purse and handed it to Topher. "Use this to find the original northwest fireplace. The message is behind the cleanout door."

"Where's that?"

With a twinkle in her eye, Madame Zaphon said, "In the cellar."

"You want me to do what?"

An hour later, Topher returned to the whiskey bar, sweaty and dirty from removing the bricks behind an old fireplace in the basement of Fraunces Tavern. He thunked a solid brass canister resembling those pneumatic tubes banks once used onto the table. Ben and Madame Zaphon abruptly stopped talking. It took several minutes to open the heavy, soot-covered container before the contents spilled onto the table: a roll of parchment and a titanium flash drive.

Madame Zaphon unrolled the paper and read it intently.

Topher tried to open the flash drive, but it was well-sealed.

"Who buried that in the bottom of a fireplace?" Topher asked.

"Either Saimon or Matija," said Madame Zaphon.

"When?"

"Today, July 1st, but in 1776."

"You mean it's been under this tavern for 235 years?"

"Exactly," said Madame Zaphon. "A bootstrapped message."

Ben asked, "What does it say?"

"What's the flash drive for?" Topher asked.

"Calibration data from the Leyden jar. What's your working knowledge of dynamical systems and—"

"—differential equations?" Topher finished the question and pointed to his head. "Been working on it. Got some books up here I'm processing."

"You'll need those skills." Madame Zaphon handed the flash drive to Topher. "Because I would like you to analyze this data. Perhaps you can discover what went wrong."

"What if I fix the problem?" Topher held up the flash drive. "You can't exactly bootstrap this into the past."

"Let that be my issue to resolve," said Madame Zaphon.

"But even if I find a solution," said Topher, "tomorrow, July 2nd, is the vote for independence."

Ben sat up straight and said, "I may not understand the science of the Bell Lift Cage and your Leyden jars, but I believe the geography hasn't changed. Even if I go back to 1776 today, I will arrive in New York City, not Philadelphia."

Topher's heart sank when he said what everyone must have been thinking: "It's too late to get you back. Ben won't make the vote for independence."

CHAPTER THIRTY

TOPHER WHITE

WELL DONE IS BETTER THAN WELL SAID

The state of nature has a law of nature to govern it, which obliges every one: and reason, which is that law, teaches all mankind, who will but consult it, that being all equal and independent, no one ought to harm another in his life, health, liberty, or possessions.

-John Locke (From the *Second Treatise of Government*, Ch. II, sec. 6, 1689)

International Mercantile Marine Company Building - 1 Broadway - New York, NY - Saturday, July 9th, 2011 - 3:30 p.m.

Topher had known the feeling of powerlessness growing up in multiple merciless foster homes, but since July 1st in Fraunces Tavern, that same sense of dread had crept into his chest because he couldn't find a bug in the Leyden jar code. His established software development skills and new knowledge of advanced mathematics were seemingly useless. It wasn't a fear of disappointing Madame Zaphon, Saimon, Matija, or even the eccentric Nikola Tesla. Ben Franklin was the reason Topher put all his focus on getting him back to 1776, even after July 2nd, when he should have cast his vote for American independence.

On July 4th at four in the morning, Topher woke in a panic, convinced the holiday would suddenly disappear because Ben hadn't gone back. He slipped out, ran across Battery Park, and waited until five thirty when the sun rose to confirm Lady Liberty was still there—no new monument to Joseph Stalin.

After a breakfast of fast food, Ben and Topher went up to Central Park and finished the day on Pier 86 atop the aircraft carrier of the Intrepid Sea, Air & Space Museum. As always, the septuagenarian had marveled at the technical and architectural advancements of New York City. Topher couldn't enjoy the 4th of July spirit. Running calculations and code through his mind while constantly pulling the compression sleeves over the scars at the edges of his wrists was all he could do.

By July 9th, Ben became less dependent on the mobility scooter and insisted on short walks, which today ended on a park bench in Bowling Green facing the fountain. He told Topher there used to be an enormous statue of King George the Third back in 1776. They erected the fence that surrounded the park to prevent the patriots from tearing it down. They sat quietly as Ben watched the pedestrians, especially women in skirts and high heels.

After Ben had gotten enough rest, they walked across the street to the penthouse apartment on 1 Broadway for an afternoon snack Ben called a tea. It was a daily ritual since they had arrived in New York City. Ben quipped it was the only thing English he still held dear. In the beginning, Topher had ordered a more traditional catered meal of cucumber sandwiches, scones, and coffee for their "Teatime," but today, Ben wanted McDonald's cheeseburgers, coffee, and milkshakes.

While they waited for the fast-food delivery, Ben tried to start a conversation about the philosophies of Plato, Aristotle, and John Locke, but Topher mindlessly nodded to be polite as he analyzed mathematical formulas on his laptop.

"Do we have any more of that bottled cream?" Ben asked. "I'd like to put it in my coffee when it arrives."

Topher said, "You finished the Baileys Irish Cream yesterday. Besides, it's more alcohol and sugar than cream."

"I wish you'd stop pressing buttons on that portfolio and engage in this very one-sided conversation. I'd like your beliefs on how natural law supersedes laws that man and the church impose upon us. Locke said, 'The state of nature has a law of nature to govern it, which obliges every one: and reason, which is that law, teaches all mankind—'"

"—who will but consult it." Topher finished the quote.

"When did you read that?"

"Flipped through it yesterday morning." Topher pointed at his bushy Afro. "It's all up here, but philosophy ain't gonna get you back to 1776."

"Mr. Jefferson used Locke's ideas when he drafted the Declaration of Independence—which must have been a success. I loved the Independence Day fireworks and bread-wrapped sausages."

"It's called a hot dog. And you have to get back to 1776 so we can continue celebrating it."

"People in your time eat canines?"

"I told you, it's just a name. Right now, all I can think about is what's going to happen if you don't get back. I also haven't heard a thing from Madame Zaphon or Saimon—no new messages in the chimney under Fraunces Tavern or in the Bowling Green subway; I've checked every day."

Ben leaned back in his chair and let the air conditioning blow across his short hair. "It gives me great pleasure to see how my electricity experiments have led to this invention of cold indoor wind. Also satisfying is seeing how my political pursuits helped create an independent America. I don't mind staying another year before going back to 1776."

"Waiting a year is the least viable option. Remember the effects of temporal delirium?"

"No. I was enjoying a cognac."

"Of course you were."

"I assume you weren't being rhetorical," said Ben. "Then enlighten me. What happens if I stay until the year 2012?"

"Hallucinations, cognitive dysfunction, insomnia, and diarrhea."

"At the same time?"

"I made up the last one," said Topher. "But you've only been here a little under a month—not sure when or if you'd show signs of decay."

"Except for the healed wound to my belly, I feel perfectly fine and see no need for haste."

Topher got a text and hoped it was Madame Zaphon, but it was the food order. He went down to pick it up, and when he returned, Ben was perusing the liquor cabinet.

"Got what you wanted," said Topher. "But I was thinking on the way up. What if we wait until federal agents stop infesting Independence Hall? Then Madame Zaphon could take you back before the symptoms start."

"That smells delicious. Did you get the frozen creamed milk?"

Topher placed the sandwiches and drinks on the table as he said, "I doubt the Feds will clear out before October because in 1776, you need to board a boat for France."

"If I may interject," said Ben. "Full stomachs would make for a much more productive discussion of—"

The ornate double doors popped open, and Madame Zaphon entered the room. Topher turned abruptly in a jolt of fright, knocking his laptop off the table, which hit the floor and cracked the screen. Behind her was a weary-looking Saimon and his equally tired partner, Matija. Lurking in the hall was a tall, thin, white man with a thick black mustache.

Topher said to Madame Zaphon, "It's been over a week. Where were you?"

"Very good to see you, Mr. White." Madame Zaphon put her white straw hat on a hook and tightened her low, sleek bun. "I trust everything went well in my absence. And, Ben, you look radiantly healthy."

"Thank you, Gabrielle," said Ben. "Tea has arrived. Please stay and join us?"

"After the day we had, it would be most welcome," said Madame Zaphon.

Saimon emerged from the kitchen with several bottles of Evian and a medical bag. He said with a horrible English accent, "Oi, Topher. You're having teatime now? What are we having?"

"Mickey D's."

"That will hardly suffice for our guest," said Madame Zaphon as she gestured to the mustached man. "I'd like to introduce Mr. Nikola Tesla."

Ben stood from his chair and extended his hand to Tesla, who recoiled as if being handed a dead cat. "Thank you for building the new port, good sir."

Tesla only stared at Ben.

"Nikola," said Madame Zaphon, "this is Benjamin Franklin, the one for whom you configured the Leyden jar that will send him back to his time."

In accented English, Tesla said, "My mother told me I was born during a lightning storm. I took up the study of electricity because of Dr. Franklin, but this does not resemble him."

"*Someone* got him a haircut," said Madame Zaphon.

"I assure you, Mr. Tesla," said Ben, "I am who she says I am. And now, if you'll excuse me, I have to use the indoor necessary."

Ben hobbled out of the room, and Topher said to Saimon, "Weren't you supposed to drop Tesla off in 1901?"

Saimon rolled up his sleeve, stuck in a syringe, and plunged the contents into his arm. Topher knew inoculations were standard practice for the Regents before and after any time jump because a disease or virus could do a lot more damage than displacing someone in a different time period. Saimon prepped several more shots and quietly whispered, "We stopped there, but no sign of Filip, the Regent protecting Tesla. Someone broke into Tesla's lab, too. Don't know what they took, but being short on time, we brought him along to keep him safe."

Topher asked, "Who's Filip?"

"He's on the Wardenclyffe Prerogative with Neja—Regents assigned to protect Tesla."

"That's not the priority at the moment," Madame Zaphon said. "It's 1776. Saimon, please inoculate Ben. I don't want him spreading something dangerous into the eighteenth century." Then to Topher: "How many brothels has he visited this week?"

Topher couldn't believe the question, especially coming from Madame Zaphon. "He's an old man. Why do you think he'd feel the urge to—"

"I'll take that as a no, then." Then to Saimon: "Give Nikola a TCB12 shot as well. He's looking peaked from two time jumps in one day."

Topher pulled his right sleeve over his wrist and asked, "When's Ben going back?"

"Soon as possible," said Madame Zaphon. "But after we've ordered some proper food and drink for this afternoon's tea."

Ben entered the room with his floral shirt opened. His belly hung over the elastic waistband of the old-man pants. "Please don't send back the meat in bread with pickles."

Topher noticed that when Ben entered the room, Tesla pulled a handkerchief from his pocket and placed it over his mouth, appearing ready to vomit.

Topher turned to Ben and said, "They're called cheeseburgers."

Ben said, "Am I going back this afternoon?"

Madame Zaphon said, "Indeed. The British are getting more anxious in New York Harbor. And those clothes will not do, Ben. You'll have to wear the clothes in which you arrived back on June 11th. And a wig."

Ben said, "Indeed, I shall miss these clothes, but I refuse to wear any wig. It irritates my scalp."

"I got you a gift," said Topher. He handed a box to Ben. He opened it. Inside was a marten fur hat.

Ben put it on his head. "This is exquisite, and very soft indeed."

"It's exactly like the one I've seen on the posters all over Philadelphia. Who knows, it might get cold when you go to France."

"Ahh, yes, this is much better. Thank you, Topher."

Madame Zaphon said, "Ben, you must wear that hat or your wig upon return."

"It'll be something for you to remember me by," said Topher.

"Doubtful I shall forget you, or any of this."

Alexander Hamilton U.S. Customs House - 1 Bowling Green - New York, NY - Saturday, July 9th, 2011 - 6:30 p.m.

In the newly bootstrapped time portal under the northwest corner of the old U.S. Custom House,

Saimon set the year on the Leyden jar to 1776 as he gave Ben directions. "On arrival, you'll feel woozy and disoriented. Billy will be there to give you an injection that will clear your head."

Ben asked, "Who's Billy?"

"Goes by Billy Lee. He's George Washington's valet."

"You mean slave," said Topher.

"He's also a Regent, tasked to be the general's personal bodyguard," said Saimon. "He'll secure this Leyden jar."

"Thank you, Mr. Saimon," said Ben.

Topher tugged at the cuffs of his sleeves and said to Ben, "Any advice or wisdom before you leave?"

"Well done is better than well said."

Saimon depressed the plunger and closed the iron door.

As the vibrations of the time portal became more intense, Ben shouted, "Another thing, Topher, and this is important."

"What is it?" Topher leaned in toward the cage as ice crystals formed on the bars.

"Do something filled with meaning and *never* piss in the wind."

CHAPTER THIRTY-ONE

BENJAMIN FRANKLIN

THE ICONOCLASM

Little strokes fell great oaks. - Benjamin Franklin (August, 1750)

Bowling Green Park - Broadway & Whitehall Street - New York, NY - Tuesday, July 9th, 1776 - 6:40 p.m.

B en's clouded mind cleared from the haze of time travel when he saw a throng of rowdy Continental soldiers marching down Broadway. He wondered, Is this a parade to celebrate my return?

Many approaching were Continental soldiers. Ben couldn't remember arriving at Fort George and it all came to his senses when the familiar scents of 1776 assaulted his nostrils: manure, garbage, and body odor. By the time he reached 1 Broadway, Ben noticed Billy at his side. For a man of only five-feet-two, he was exceptionally strong and sharply dressed in a red turban and a pressed blue uniform dotted with brass buttons.

Ben looked up at the two-story mansion and mused, "This should be much taller."

"No, Dr. Franklin," said Billy. "This is Archibald Kennedy's home, but General Washington took it over and made it his headquarters after Mr. Kennedy fled. The one you left in 2011 won't be built until 1884. You've got to keep moving. The shot I gave you will take effect shortly."

In the small park across from the Kennedy Mansion, soldiers climbed the iron fence surrounding the statue of King George the Third on a horse. "What's happened to the fountain?"

Billy said, "General Washington ordered a reading of the Declaration of Independence to the troops, and now they're pretty juiced."

"General Washington gave them juice?" Ben asked.

"They're excited. Perhaps some are in their altitudes."

"I could use a drink myself. What's the date?"

"The same, July 9th," said Billy.

Ben, still feeling disoriented from having time traveled from 2011, said, "I missed the vote for Independence. They set it for July 2nd."

"Yes, but they didn't need you for it. Enough Pennsylvania delegates were present to vote, so it passed. I'll explain later, but you need to get inside and recover." Billy reached for the door handle, but a large Irishman throwing a rope over the statue distracted Ben.

Ben asked, "Who is that large man?"

"That's Hercules Mulligan, a local tailor and patriot," said Billy. "That young man in the uniform next to him is his friend, Alexander Hamilton."

Ben stood in the doorway and watched the soldiers grab the ropes on both sides and pull at the giant lead iconoclasm. It didn't take long before the statue tumbled from its marble pedestal onto the grass inside the iron fence. Minutes before, the statue of King George the Third had stood above the people. Now it was on its side, surrounded by the citizens of a newly independent nation.

Pride replaced the disorientation Ben felt from time-traveling. He approached the fence unsteadily, then smiled down at the statue of a fallen king.

Alexander Hamilton shouted, "Get the smiths to break it apart! We can melt it down for musket balls, huzzah!"

The other soldiers answered with deafening replies of huzzah!

Ben placed his hand on the young soldier's shoulder and said, "Excellent idea, Mr. Hamilton."

"We'll give the statue back to the Regulars in pieces," said Hamilton. "Through the barrels of our muskets!"

"Dr. Franklin." Billy tugged at Ben's arm. It's not safe out here. "General Washington will greet you at the Kennedy mansion. Please, I beg you to get inside."

"Not just yet. I'm enjoying the revelry," said Ben.

Billy stared intently at an opened pocket watch with a face that glowed like Topher's ear-phone and, "Something is off - two bogies."

Ben heard the rumble of hooves coming down Broadway and turned to see George Washington, the 44-year-old Commander-in-Chief of the Continental Army, riding a most majestic gray horse. Later, he learned the horse's name was Blueskin. General Washington slowed to a trot and halted short of Ben and Billy. He dismounted, and Ben didn't recall George as being so tall.

George removed his gloves and said, "Dr. Franklin, nobody sent a dispatch to announcing your arrival."

"I appeared quite suddenly," said Ben.

Billy stepped in closer and whispered, "Your Excellency, the Continental Congress sent Dr. Franklin on a clandestine mission to discuss supply lines."

Ben thought, *What a brilliant young man.*

"It will be of great interest to discuss that," said George. "This army urgently needs supplies."

Ben got closer to George and said, "I've also gotten a view of the future that I must provide before I return to Philadelphia. Information that will prepare you for what is coming."

Billy looked at Ben with wide eyes that clearly conveyed: You *really* shouldn't do that.

"They have informed me you wrote the Declaration of Independence, Doctor Franklin," said George. "As you can see, it's left my men in an excitable state."

"It was a Virginian who drafted it, Mr. Thomas Jefferson. I provided only minor edits because I was infirmed."

"Indeed," said George. "It's fitting that a Virginian wrote it." He gestured to the empty plinth where the statue of King George the Third once proudly stood. "Dr. Franklin, I must speak plainly."

"As I will with you," said Ben.

George said, "Writing the Declaration was a less dangerous task. You didn't have muskets and cannon pointed at you while drafting it."

"Not in the least. In fact, we had air conditioning." Ben smiled inwardly because they had composed the document 235 years in the future. He wanted to reveal all he had learned in the majestic Rose Main Reading Room of the New York Public Library about the battles of the Revolutionary War. He knew the trials ahead for George Washington would be long and arduous, and it required another Seven Years' War before they were ultimately victorious.

Above the noise of the soldiers and Patriots celebrating, Ben gazed into George's blue-gray eyes and shouted, "You are correct, General. The Declaration of Independence is only words on paper written by a young Virginian. Now, sir, it's time for an experienced Virginian to lead the army in a war of Revolution to defend it from the—"

Billy interrupted, "This is best discussed inside, General Washington and Dr. Franklin,"

"You're staring at that watch again," George said to Billy. "I do not understand your preoccupation with time."

"Got an uneasy feeling right now, Your Excellency," said Billy.

"Another of your premonitions?" said George. "American troops stand all around and the loyalists have been driven out. I'm well-guarded and feel quite safe."

Ben winked at Billy and addressed George: "Your Excellency, I do feel the need for respite, despite the festivities."

As Billy led Blueskin towards the Kennedy Mansion, the throng of soldiers and citizens parted like the Red Sea. Midway there, Billy stopped and said without pointing, "Your Excellency, do you recognize that woman holding a fan? She's in the hat with peacock feathers." Billy flipped open opened his pocket watch and seemed alarmed.

"Where?" asked George.

Billy nodded in her direction and said, "Yonder, at the front door of the Watts House. Is she the lady of the house?"

Ben said, "Quite fashionably dressed for such an occasion."

"I've never seen her before, and the house has been vacant since we arrived," said George.

"Not a friendly," said Billy.

Ben sensed the lady had noted their attention because she abruptly descended the stairs and walked hurriedly north on Broadway. He turned to George and said, "Perhaps she's taking in the spectacle."

Billy said, "Stay frosty - one heading north, the other stationary, hundred fifty meters south of my twenty." He then slapped the hind quarter of Blueskin, who whinnied and reared up instantly.

A musket ripped open Blueskin's spine. The horse seemed to scream in pain as its rear legs wobbled under the weight.

Ben looked to his left, to where the shot originated, and determined it came from the Northwest bastion of Fort George.

Billy let the paralyzed horse flop to the street and shouted, "Let's get inside before the sniper can reload!" He grabbed the arm of General Washington and ran.

Ben limped several feet behind. It was difficult to keep up.

Before George and Billy reached the first step of 1 Broadway, Ben heard a cannon blast come from the Hudson River. Was this a coordinated British attack in response to the Declaration of Independence?

A deafening explosion overhead stopped Ben's hobbling approach. He looked up and saw the roof shatter, splintering debris in all directions.

J.M. RASINSKE

   Ben Franklin turned away and something hit the
back of his head

THE END

TO BE CONTINUED in Volume 2 - REVOLUTION

ACKNOWLEDGMENTS

A true legend of fiction, Walter Mosley, inspired me to write this after I read *This Year You Write Your Novel* (2007). I thanked him personally in New York City at Thrillerfest 2018 for his role in making this book a reality.

The preponderance of acknowledgement goes to the Deskimo Brothers: Scott Blackburn, J.G. Hetherton, Russell W. Johnson, Philip Kimbrough, and Eryk Pruitt. Your support, input, and fellowship transformed this novel into what it is today. I am truly humbled to have received counsel from such exceptional authors.

Thanks and love to my father, Michael Rasinske.

Dawn Marie, thank you for the grace and patience you've shown throughout this jagged journey to publication.

To Samuel, Owen, Emmett, and Ainsley, my children. You are all precious gifts from God. I appreciate all the encouragement and goodwill given to me as I have strived to model how you should always pursue your dreams, regardless of your age or barriers this life inevitably brings.

Author's Notes

About the Title

Inspiration for the title of this series, A FOREST OF GIANT OAKS, comes from a speech given by a 29-year-old lawyer 23 years before he became President of the United States — Excerpt From: *The Perpetuation of Our Political Institutions*: Address Before the Young Men's Lyceum of Springfield, Illinois by Abraham Lincoln on January 27, 1838 (bold added for emphasis):

> I do not mean to say, that the scenes of the revolution *are now* or *ever will* be entirely forgotten; but that like every thing else, they must fade upon the memory of the world, and grow more and more

dim by the lapse of time. In history, we hope, they will be read of, and recounted, so long as the bible shall be read;-- but even granting that they will, their influence *cannot be* what it heretofore has been. Even then, they *cannot be* so universally known, nor so vividly felt, as they were by the generation just gone to rest. At the close of that struggle, nearly every adult male had been a participator in some of its scenes. The consequence was, that of those scenes, in the form of a husband, a father, a son or brother, a *living history* was to be found in every family-- a history bearing the indubitable testimonies of its own authenticity, in the limbs mangled, in the scars of wounds received, in the midst of the very scenes related--a history, too, that could be read and understood alike by all, the wise and the ignorant, the learned and the unlearned.--But *those* histories are gone. They *can* be read no more forever. They *were* a fortress of strength; but, what invading foeman could *never do*, the silent artillery of time *has done*; the leveling of its walls. They are gone.--They *were* **a forest of giant oaks**; but the all-resistless hurricane has swept over them, and left only, here and there, a lonely trunk, despoiled of its verdure, shorn of its foliage; unshading and unshaded, to murmur in a few gentle breezes, and to combat with its mutilated limbs, a few more ruder storms, then to sink, and be no more.

Why it's Germane Today

Both the Committee of Five and Lincoln have departed from this Earth, as well as everyone who knew them personally. These influential, yet flawed people, remain as giant oaks in our republic's history to many Americans. Thanks for reading my small contribution to help that forest be relevant and relatable.